Captain Justin Harris galloped down the line to inspect his troopers. He was worried: this was Mexico, and the U.S. Cavalry had no business being here. He passed the last man in his troop and halted, and saw Lieutenant Ben Hannibal a few yards away staring at him. There was a plea in Hannibal's eyes: Justin Harris wished he had an answer to it or had not seen it.

In a moment they would ride over the crest and attack. There was nothing he could say to Ben Hannibal: Ben Hannibal would have to fight today and perhaps out of the crucible of rifle combat he would draw his own decisions. Even death, in its way, was a decision.

# BUGLE

# AND

# SPUR

# Frank O'Brian

**BALLANTINE BOOKS** · **NEW YORK**
An Intext Publisher

SBN 345-02077-4-075

First Printing: November, 1966
Second Printing: November, 1970

Cover Art by Ronald Lesser

Printed in Canada

BALLANTINE BOOKS, INC.
101 Fifth Avenue, New York, N.Y. 10003

# BUGLE

# AND

# SPUR

# 1

The silver stripe of the coach road curled down into the desert. The light brougham stagecoach kicked up a grit cloud that yellowed the sky and matted men's faces and hung behind them on shimmering heat undulations. Here and there they clattered past a gray-green clump of brush, no bigger than a hat. One of the mounted troopers pinched sand from his eyes and squinted downhill to the vast flow of the desert —the narrow green-belted curve of the Smoke River, then the plain. The trooper said, "Four hours to home. Calm as a horse trough down there. Won't see no Apaches today."

"Don't complain, Hoag."

"Not me, Captain."

Justin Harris went past at a lope and took the lead position. Behind him the ten troopers swayed around the lurching coach like mosquitoes. Sun-charred hands rested on carbine buttstocks, indifferent to the searing metal heat. Justin Harris was a dust-slurred scarecrow, the yellow stripes down his pants matted into the land's universal sand color. He felt raw and irritable, the beleaguered captain of a tiny ship of men swaying across the wastes.

The coach bucked and pitched with a dry racket. They broke into the cottonwood shade and halted by the river; in a bad humor Justin Harris watched his men tumble to the bank and drink lustily. The two horse holders looked on spitefully. A civilian passenger stepped down from inside the coach and blinked. "Can't be far from here to hell, Captain."

"Not far at all," Justin Harris said.

Trooper Hoag came back from the river. "Dig down a few feet, you be right there. It's a little cooler than here."

"I can believe that." The civilian's shirt was open down to the navel; he had left his suit coat inside the coach. Sweat ran free down his face. He called up to the driver, "Mind if I ride with you awhile? Maybe the wind will help."

"Wind's like a hot God-damned saw," said the driver, and spat tobacco juice over the side. "But suit yourself."

The civilian had a drink from the river and made an effort of climbing to the driver's seat. Justin Harris checked the cinch of his horse. Someone cursed. The shade was tempting, but Justin Harris turned to the detail's sergeant. "Mount them up."

He did not watch. He could hear the creak of saddles, the jingle of bridle bits. He put his horse into the river and splashed across the shallows and cut away from the trees. The heat hit him a reeling blow.

The desert was given to fits of temper. He had seen temperatures whip up or down by forty-degree intervals in a matter of hours. A wind would come, shatter the stillness, destroy, and go on. A powder-dry arroyo would become a torrent and dry up again, all in the space of a day.

The desert unrolled toward the mountains far away: soil packed into hard, crumbled powder by a sun stripped naked of vapor. Here and there a gray plant clung to life, spine-armored, stunted, defiant.

Justin Harris glanced over his shoulder and fell back to close up the detail. Trooper Hoag said, "Hundred and twenty in the shade."

"What shade, Trooper?"

"That's it, Captain. But a man can wait. Winter come, we'll have easy duty again. I always wait for winter."

Harris pushed his hatbrim up and squeezed sweat from his forehead. Mica particles and pyrites lay in the ground, set like diamonds in a brooch on a pale throat, sparkling like sunlight on ocean crests; the sun was brass, and the little slivers shot painfully against the exposed surfaces of his slitted eyes.

Someone said scornfully, "Apache country."

"Give it back. Let them have it."

They crossed a low hump and had their view of Fort Dragoon. It blended distantly into the weathered hue of the desert. The civilian called down from his seat, and Justin Harris waved a lethargic hand in acknowledgment. Trooper Hoag said, "That gent from the Indian Bureau again, Captain?"

"That's right."

"Jesus. Another one of those."

Harris was too uncomfortable to smile; he might have. His elbows and knees and Adam's apple were sharp against the skin; his body was too long; he had a gangling gauntness. His face had broken angles, all of them brittle, like the creases in old leather, but he was twenty-seven and by far the youngest field-grade officer in the Twenty-sixth.

They walked their horses through the post settlement; the coach driver rested a foot against his brake handle. They passed the fringe of Agency Indian huts. There was a stink of sun-drying hides. One of Harris's troopers cried hoarsely: "Juanita—where the hell are you?"

They crossed a row of open-front saloons; no one could miss the outwashing odor of stale beer. A woman appeared in a cantina doorway, and the same trooper said, "Honey, open me a God-damned keg of beer—I be right down."

The sergeant said, "That's enough, buck."

Justin Harris drew abreast a small adobe, and a slender dark woman came from the shadows; she stood in the sun and looked up at him, neither smiling nor speaking. Justin Harris nodded to her with reserved courtesy and passed her by. The woman stepped inside, away from the rising dust. The coach squeaked and rumbled, and Harris could hear the civilian talking to the driver. They crossed a barren flat where a fat Apache woman bent, spreading dirty blankets over ant-hills. The big red ants would eat lice and vermin; then she would wash the blankets, unmindful of ant stings. The woman brushed strands of black hair from her swollen face and regarded the procession inscrutably until Harris's sergeant uttered a Spanish obscenity and the woman grinned.

Two Apaches in big cowboy hats squatted in the shade by a mule corral, playing mumblety-peg with a wicked long knife that glittered fragmentarily as it tumbled. The civilian on the coach watched curiously; the man's knuckles were white from gripping the edge of his pitching, hard seat.

Fort Dragoon had no stockade. There was an unfenced

scatter of low buildings laid out in a loose square around a
wetted-down flat of earth. Beyond the quadrangle squatted
the stables and corrals, along a dry creek banked with brush.
Past the sutler's store the main gate stood alone like a forgotten Roman arch, with a faded wooden sign hung from
rusting chains. The road under it was worn deep into hard-
pan ruts.

"Hot as Juanita's pants."

Someone laughed without energy. At the far end of the
parade ground the flagstaff towered; the flag hung listless,
as dust-matted and gray as the rest.

Laundress huts marked the road from settlement to fort.
The depot lay at the near edge of the settlement; the stage
halted, bouncing fore and aft on leather springs. The civilian
climbed down and made the motions of dusting himself off.
"My rump's stiff as a floorboard." He threw his head back
to look up at Justin Harris.

"I'll just wash a few pounds of dust off, Captain. Pick
me up in an hour—is that the hotel? Good God. Well, thanks
for the escort. Tell the major I'll be along."

Justin Harris touched the brim of his campaign hat and
wheeled away from the depot. The detail rode past the
regimental offices toward the stables; Justin Harris dismounted by the headquarters office and passed the reins of his
horse to a trooper. Harris climbed the porch, and the detail,
gathering high spirits, drummed away; the sergeant's bellowing voice trailed back from the stables.

The regimental sergeant major stood by the door with his
belly a perilous arc out over his waistband. His shoulders
were thrown well back to offset the displacement of mass.
His eyes were bloodshot; they were always bloodshot. "Easy
trip, Captain?"

"Hot but easy. Any news, McCracken?"

"Not to speak of."

McCracken never saluted. Perhaps he felt it would require
too much effort. Harris returned the salute McCracken had
not offered, and went inside.

The major was writing, inkwell and blotter at his elbow.
He wrote with a deliberate hand. He poised the quill pen

and looked up with a quick smile that came and went. "Take your hat off or you'll scrape the doorway. Good trip, Justin?"

"Tolerable. Simpson's at the hotel."

"Oh, God."

"Yes, sir. He'll be along. I'm to pick him up in an hour."

"Oh, God," Major Cole said again. Behind him in a dry wood frame hung his diploma—Warner H. Cole, U. S. Military Academy, Class of 1847.

"I'm putting in for a transfer to hell," the major said. He signed an order with a flourish. "Anything to report?"

"No Apache sign on the route that we could see."

"All right. Well?"

"Well, sir?"

"You've got an hour. Take a bath. Get drunk. Find a woman. Harass your men. Challenge the adjutant to a duel. *Do* something—get the hell out of here and amuse yourself, damn it."

Harris was sure his face might crack if he smiled. He only nodded and went out.

Sergeant Major McCracken had not moved. On the porch he stood rooted, watching the listless dismounted drill of a column of "B" Troop veterans. The sun hung midway across a cobalt afternoon. It stung Justin Harris's leather face. He could hear the crunch of the marching column of fours, muffled and steady; now and then the drill sergeant croaked a husky command and the column changed direction. McCracken growled, "Sloppy."

"How long since you've marched close order, McCracken?"

"I learned how before I quit," McCracken replied.

Footing was loose; the earth was caked and crumbly. Over the flat roofs of Bachelor Officers' Quarters, Harris could make out the blue serrates of the Sangre range. That was sixty miles away and rugged, but only a prelude to the Sierra Grande, across the border.

Harris dipped into the hanging clay *olla* with its long-handled metal cup. He offered it to McCracken. The sergeant major refused, and Harris drank the vessel dry in a gulp. He hung the cup on the rope net that suspended the *olla*. "Is that Ben Hannibal's troop?"

"I expect it is."

Harris watched the pale plume of dust, miles away on the desert. "He's in a hurry."

"That don't need to mean anything."

"Maybe." Harris took the cup again, drank half, and splashed his hands wet; he scrubbed his face. "Camped at Arroyo Seco last night. I saw three fish swimming upstream backwards to keep the dust out of their eyes."

McCracken laughed politely. Harris said, "Sorry. I guess it's too God-damned hot for a laugh."

"Almost hot enough for an Apache," McCracken agreed. "Here comes the mail."

Dust and noise preceded the mail coach. It pitched through the main gate, a splintered old hack escorted by a sergeant and five troopers. The coach arrived like an untamed horse at the adjutant's office next door and bucked to a halt just long enough for the driver to toss down the mailbag and bawl, "No freight—no passengers," and then it wheeled improbably toward the ugly town.

"Now," McCracken said, "that was just two wasted words. Who in hell would take passage to this tropical paradise in the middle of the rainy season, I'm asking you."

The adjutant's corporal walked out and took the mailbag into the office. McCracken yanked up his trousers, hooked thumbs in his suspenders, and backed against the wall; he waited until the corporal appeared again with a handful of letters, one of which was still sealed. According to the protocol of rank, McCracken stood where he was and let the corporal come to him. Harris had another drink from the *olla*, trying to stir up the energy to leave the porch shade. The corporal handed the major's mail to McCracken, said, "Fresh beer in today," and went back to his office next door.

McCracken licked his lips and took the mail inside with a great sigh and a display of reluctance. When he came back to the porch, he said, "Dust growing under Rincon Peak. Lieutenant Hannibal appears to have a burr under his saddle, don't he? He's a good one-bar, that one. Didn't take him long at all to settle down to size."

Justin Harris said, "Don't let him see your good opinion."

"No. We wouldn't want to be swelling the lieutenant's

head, would we? But then again, why should the lieutenant be valuing *my* opinions, Captain?"

"Hell, McCracken," Justin Harris said. He tugged the hat down over his eyes and thrust himself into the sunlight; he went toward Officers' Row with slow, long strides.

He washed and changed into a clean uniform and glanced at the clock; he still had twenty minutes before the man from the Indian Bureau would be ready. Harris put on a garrison cap and walked out onto the parade ground. The drilling "B" Troop soldiers were dispersing into the barracks. McCracken still was on the office porch, standing in slow-moving shade with his hooded attention on the approaching dust banner of Lt. Ben Hannibal's hurrying band of horsemen. The patrol was coming home after a three-day swing through a wide sector of brutal wilderness. They would settle their horses and stop by the sutler's for a beer to sustain them on their way to the bawdy houses and cantinas of the post settlement. In a few days their turn would again come to ride out. It was all part of a pattern without change; the army was like Sergeant Major McCracken, as immutable as the granite mountains yonder.

A paint detail, five men without shirts, rounded a corner carrying buckets and brushes, and readied themselves to whitewash the adjutant's porch rails. Justin Harris left the door of his quarters, yanking down his blue cap, and walked loosely toward the water trough near the main gate. Pete Rubio was bent there, splashing water over his head, the reins of his ugly horse draped over one arm.

Pete Rubio snorted and shook his head like a wet dog. He ran fingers through dripping straight hair that fell to his shoulders Apache-fashion. Chief of Scouts, Rubio wore buckskin trousers and a blue cavalry blouse, testimony to his divided half-breed world. When Harris approached within twenty paces, Rubio turned alertly.

"I see you got back with the great son-of-a-bitching white father."

"Any sign in the Sangres, Pete?"

"There's always sign. Don't mean nothing. Run across tracks ten hours old—they could be eighty mile away by now."

"Or looking down your throat," Harris said.

"Nobody looks down my throat without I know it," Pete Rubio said without bravado.

"Offhand, I can't think of anybody who'd want to, Pete."

Rubio's wide mouth cracked into a smile. "You ain't so damned pretty yourself, Justin," he said, and walked away, leading his horse. Justin Harris took a small, abstracted pleasure—he was the only officer on Fort Dragoon who could elicit a break in expression from the Chief of Scouts. Pete Rubio was customarily the most suspicious and taciturn of men.

Harris felt grit on his hands—he had washed them perhaps five minutes ago. He dampened them under the trough spigot and let them hang dripping. Up on the major's porch Sergeant Major McCracken held a desultory conversation with the adjutant's corporal. The ring of the corporal's easy laughter floated across the compound. It was evidence enough that the afternoon was waning, that the heat was dissipating. No one ever laughed before four o'clock.

Harris had a single impatient thought about the unsatisfactory routine of life and decided it was time to collect the man from the Indian Bureau. Without pleasure he tramped into town and kicked his boot heels on the hotel steps to dislodge dust before he went inside. He had to accustom his eyes to the dim lobby. The clerk was its only occupant. The clerk was middle-aged and bald and tired; life had passed him by, unnoticed. Justin Harris said, "Tell Mr. Simpson I'm here."

In a little while the civilian came out of the dark corridor, wearing a bottle-green coat. They went out on the porch, and Simpson said, "Christ, look at that dust." His boots were polished to a high shine. "I've ordered a buggy. What's holding them up?"

"Nothing happens very fast around here," Justin Harris said, faintly irritated by the civilian's failure even to try to adapt.

"What kind of man is Major Cole?"

"A good officer."

After a moment Simpson said, "Is that all you've got to say?"

"What's the use of idle conversation? My opinion won't mean anything to you. You'll get your own idea of him when you meet him."

The man from the Indian Bureau studied Harris. "You talk more like a cowboy than an officer."

It was still hot enough; Harris didn't summon the energy to think up a reply. A buckboard rolled up, driven by a small Mexican with an immense moustache. Harris climbed in after Simpson—dislike disinclined him to offer Simpson the courtesy of the outside seat. Mr. Simpson sat uncomfortably between Harris and the Mexican, with nothing to grip. The buckboard was made of gray splintered wood. It swayed away from the hotel behind its single dray horse, and by the time they reached the major's office, Mr. Simpson's fine boots had a coat of filmed dust.

The hack squeaked when its passengers got down. Harris stood stoically by until Simpson, with a sharp, angry cough, reached into his pocket and paid the silent Mexican. Sergeant Major McCracken, on the porch, smiled gently; Simpson did not see that. He slapped at the fine overlay of dust on his green coat. The face, normally sallow, was windburned; the lips were cracked.

The buckboard rattled away, making dust. Mr. Simpson looked very dryly at Justin Harris and went inside without a word. Harris climbed into the shade. The sergeant major winked solemnly. Harris could see the civilian walking across the empty outer office in a stiff-jointed manner, as if the desert dust had gotten into his joints.

"Getting a little breeze out here," McCracken said. He inclined his head toward the office with a low laugh. "That fellow's a windy, ain't he? I hate to see a man the cut of Major Cole have to kowtow to a dude with pink skin and a soft belly."

Harris could hear voice tones from the inner office. Mr. Simpson talked, and the major responded in a reasoning way. Presently Simpson came to the door, looked around, and went back inside, closing the door after him. It prompted McCracken's little smile.

Harris sweated in the shade. He had no place to go just now, and interest in the advancing dust of Lt. Ben Hannibal's

detachment held him on the porch. He had a fair idea what
was transpiring in the major's office. He knew Mr. Simpson
—knew him without ever having seen the man before. Indian
Bureau representatives were all cut from the same stripe;
their idealism was corrupted by innocence.

A narrow band of sunlight crept onto the veranda, driving
Harris and McCracken nearer the door. Harris felt mild
sympathy for the major. They all resented the periodic Indian
Bureau visitors—intruders from the East, blinded by inexperi-
ence and ignorance, travelers from a far world trying to set
things right with a smile, a flourish, or a pompous warning.

This incident, now—the Rice family massacre perpetrated
by Togomasai's bunch. Mr. Simpson would be horrified by
the rape of the wife, the scalping of Rice's vaqueros. Rice
had been tied down, cruciform, over an anthill. Mr. Simpson
would swallow. "You can be assured I'll take this story back
to Washington, Major. It may put a little backbone into some
of my colleagues who believe in mollycoddling these sav-
ages."

The civilian would go home and give the politicians a report. He would see only the incident, not its cause. The
Rice deaths could partly be blamed on Rice's own blind
pride; Rice had known Togomasai's gang had jumped the
reservation; Rice had time to take refuge. He had had a
choice. But that fact wouldn't fit Mr. Simpson's concept. It
would not matter to Mr. Simpson that where the Apaches
were involved, there had to be two parties to an atrocity.

Mr. Simpson's people had no great interest in the truth.
Perhaps that was just as well; Justin Harris had reached a
point where concern with truth had no importance. But it
was not the same with men from the Indian Bureau. Façade
was their way of life. With idle, uncaring speculation, Justin
Harris thought of the tempting ideas that must be going
through the major's head:

A line trooper earns twelve dollars a month, Mr. Simpson.
It may strike you it's hard to get a good man to work for
that. The army you've paid for—it's a litter of mongrel pups.
Some unweaned. Hill people, stevedores, slum rats, farmers,
immigrants who don't know or don't care what they're here
for. Men on the run, hiding behind an anonymous uniform.

Probably every sixth or seventh man on this garrison has his face on "Wanted" fliers somewhere. We have no glory to offer, Mr. Simpson. No dedicated troops, no hope for promotion, no way to bring forces up to authorized strength on the pinched pennies the War Department begrudges us. Bad weather, food that gives a man the scurvy, wages a Mexican vaquero would spit at. A clever enemy and poor chances for decisive combat victories. The Apache cuts and runs—we nibble at him; it's all we can do. We'll erode them away eventually, and they know it, but they fight anyway. Who knows why? For dignity, for pride, for honor, or maybe for pure cussedness. But we're all crippled. The Apache is far better equipped to fight here than we are. We're interlopers, still learning the basic rules of survival. It's his home, and he knows it the way you know your own house in Arlington, Mr. Simpson, so that you can find the toilet at midnight without lighting a lamp. It's tribute to our discipline that we even hold our own."

A dust devil whirled in the shape of a tornado out on the flats beyond town. The murmur of voices came through the thin door from the office. Sergeant Major McCracken had a rigid smile. He rubbed his paunch absently. A ragged line of soldiers crawled across the compound, tramping its winding shadow into the earth. Mr. Simpson came outside unhappily and gave the fort a curious look. Justin Harris said, "If you like, I'll get you a buckboard."

"I'll walk." The man from the Indian Bureau went away without further comment. The shine was gone from his boots.

McCracken let the stillness hang for a while. Then he spoke. "Lieutenant Hannibal's at a lope."

"It can't be too serious. He'd have sent a dispatch rider."

"I reckon."

Major Cole appeared from the office. Hatless, he shaded his eyes with his palm. The sun was lowering; it reached waist level at the doorway. The major appeared troubled. He turned a shoulder to the two others and dipped into the water *olla* and drank. He said, "Hot," and meticulously twisted water from his moustache.

"Hot and close," said McCracken. "There was a breeze, but it left."

"You've got a loose tongue, McCracken."

"Sorry, Major." But McCracken did not look chastened.

Mr. Simpson was a small shape nearing the hotel. The major said, "He had a long, uncomfortable trip and a useless one. Those people don't seem able to distinguish between one Indian and another. It didn't make sense to him that Togomasai is just as much an outlaw in the Apache tribes as he is in white country. He didn't see why you couldn't make a treaty. How do you make treaties with outlaws?"

"Sign it with a Springfield bullet," McCracken said.

"We'll never have them in our sights," Major Cole said. "Walk up the row with me, Justin."

They left the porch shoulder to shoulder. The major said, "Is that Hannibal?"

"Yes."

"He's in a rush, isn't he?" He took out a cigar and gave it a glance; preoccupied, he put the cigar back in his pocket and buttoned the flap. "I hope he's had no trouble this time out."

"You sound jaded," Justin Harris said.

"Do I? Well, then, maybe I am."

They passed the Officers' Mess and turned in at the gate of the major's small house. "Too hot to go inside—let's sit on the porch." There were three chairs; the major took the rocker.

Justin Harris said, "Mr. Simpson get under your skin?"

"A little. But it's something else. I had sealed orders from Sheridan today. My transfer. You'll have a new commanding officer in three weeks' time."

A gust of voiced breath escaped Harris. "I'm sorry."

"I know. Thank you."

"It's a rotten turn."

"Maybe. I can't question it. Keep it under your hat until I make the announcement." One corner of the major's mouth turned up. "Mueller would be upset if he knew I'd told you first. I wish I'd had some way to transfer him at the same time—give you a crack at the adjutant's job."

"I'd just as soon keep my troop," said Harris. His long face was wooden. He studied the major's moustache gravely. "Is it going to be Mallory?"

"How did you guess that?"

"Rumors."

"Maybe that's my trouble. I'm always the last one to know things. Yes, I'm afraid it is Mallory."

"Well, then, I'm sorry."

"You said that before."

"I meant it differently before."

The major said, "In the long run none of it makes any difference."

A small white cloud scudded past the sun, shadowing the seated men for a few minutes. The major said, "Mueller will keep his job as adjutant unless Mallory brings someone of his own."

"I understand Mallory usually travels alone."

"Then you're stuck with Mueller and Mallory both. I can't imagine a worse combination, if you don't mind my frankness."

"Maybe it won't be so bad."

"You have an easygoing way of taking things, Justin. I wish I had it."

Justin Harris stretched his legs out before him and tipped his head forward; his long jaw lay along his chest. He brooded upon his boots. On a gust of wind he caught the muffled drum of hoofbeats, and when he looked up he could see Ben Hannibal's detachment of eighteen soldiers slowly emerging from their own dust cloud. The detail circled the town and rode past the huts which the army chose to list as laundresses' quarters; one of Hannibal's men shouted to a girl, and the girl waved back, pushing hair out of her eyes, watching the troopers come in. Lt. Ben Hannibal paused by the headquarters office and passed a few words with Mc-Cracken; the lieutenant nodded and swung toward the major's house. The troopers dismounted and shambled into the shade of the stables. Lusty oaths issued from the place.

Lt. Ben Hannibal saluted before he got down; he loosened the cinch and stepped up on the porch. Neither Major Cole nor Justin Harris bothered to rise. Ben Hannibal batted his campaign hat against his leg, clouding the region with powder dust. He gave a quick impression of a wide but bony young face, a studious and slightly bleak expression, wind-

burned skin caked with sand. Harris said, "If you grew your
hair out, you'd look more like Custer."

"Shut up, Justin." Ben Hannibal was in a poor mood.

The major said, "Well, Ben?"

"We're back, Major, as you see."

"Nobody hurt. You hurried home."

"Yes, sir." There was a quiet interval. Harris inclined his
head toward the empty chair, and Hannibal settled into it,
sitting up straight. His eyes were dark-rimmed, and there
was dust grit on his lips. His voice started up, low and husky.

"We went down past the forks and camped outside Spanish Flat the first night. Crossed trails with Lieutenant Sandin
—half a troop escorting some freight wagons."

"They came in yesterday."

"No trouble, I hope, sir?"

"No. No trouble."

Ben Hannibal screwed his hat around in his hands. "About
three in the morning a prospector rode into our bivouac like
a demon. Gave his name as Keenan. He told me a gang of
Mimbreños had jumped his camp that sundown. It seems
Keenan and his brother and some others were working a
claim right below Santa Rosa Peak. I got the detail mounted,
and Keenan led us up there. We got there about ten yesterday morning, found three bodies—two shot and scalped. By
the arrow markings my scout judged it was some of Togomasai's bunch. The third prospector, Keenan's brother, must
have put up a good fight—they'd roasted him on a stake
before they took off his hair. There was a lot of blood on
the ground. We didn't find any Indian dead, but they probably had some—they always cart them away for burying.
They'd cooked one of the miners' burros, and it looked as
though they'd had a feast there. They took the rest of the
stock with them—one mule, three burros. I had Mingus
scouting for me. He said the Indians hadn't pulled out more
than two hours ahead of us, so I went after them. Some
of them were on foot, and I thought maybe we'd have a
chance to catch up. I figured to leave a burial detail, but
Keenan said they were his kin and his friends and he wanted
to take care of that himself. He was standoffish, Keenan—
made a few remarks about the army. Never there when they

need us, and why haven't we run Togomasai's gang down by now—that kind of thing. He used some strong language. I let it pass, considering, and the last I saw of him, he was digging with a pickax. That's pretty hard ground up there, mainly rocks."

Justin Harris said in a tinder-dry voice, "Maybe he struck it rich digging graves—who knows?" His throat felt taut, and he wished he had a drink of water.

Ben Hannibal ignored him. "Togomasai knows how to move, with or without horses. We chased them the rest of the day. Mingus couldn't tell whether it was Togomasai or some younger buck leading the pack—we never got that close. They stuck together most of the day, straight south past the Mogul Rim, around the east end of the Piedras. About six last night we got into the hills by Ten Springs, and the tracks split up, men afoot going one way and pony tracks another, and then they divided again, going into different canyons, ones and twos. We singled out a pair of tracks and followed right up to the border, got there about an hour after dark. We camped and turned back this morning."

Ben Hannibal straightened out his mangled hat. "I'm damned sorry I haven't got anything better to report. I was half a mind to chase them across the border into Mexico, clear up to those Sierra rancherias. They'd butchered three men, and I was good and mad."

"That would have been violating the Mexican treaty," the major murmured.

"Yes, sir."

"You did well. You did the best you could." The major stirred. "Maybe they'll put that on our tombstones—'they did their best.' All right, Ben, write up your report after evening mess."

Justin Harris said lazily, "Get cleaned up and I'll buy you a beer."

Ben Hannibal got out of the chair and saluted vaguely and left. The major maintained a judiciously blank expression until he was gone. "I suppose Sheridan's orders are the right ones. God knows I seem to have made a dismal failure of this campaign."

"Not your fault, Major," said Justin Harris.

Major Cole's shoulders lifted slightly and dropped. "I hope Drew Mallory doesn't crush the spring out of that boy. He's got the makings. Well, in a little while it won't be my headache any more. But you can't forget who your friends are, can you?"

The sun was a bitter red disk. Justin Harris made no answer.

## 2

Justin Harris was gaunt and sharp-jointed, but he had superb coordination, and in cool weather there were sometimes lines of casual good humor around his eyes. He hooked his boot on the rail of the sutler's bar and sucked foam from the top of his beer mug. Beside him, Ben Hannibal stood, young and sturdy, complaining in an idle, absent voice.

"I wasn't meant to be a cavalryman. It just wasn't in the cards. I feel like I'm split up to my collarbone—maybe that McClellan saddle's comfortable for a horse, but for me it's a torture rack. When nobody's looking, I stuff the damned slot with a wadded towel."

"How are your feet?"

"Blisters."

"Then you're better off in the cavalry."

"No. I belong in the artillery. I figured it all out on the way home today. I'd like to be the fellow in charge of firing twenty-one-gun salutes whenever a general retires in Washington."

"And between times?" Harris said.

"Cards, whiskey, and women."

"You're a toy soldier, that's all."

"I'm no soldier at all," Ben Hannibal said, and swallowed

his beer with distaste. "Lets go into town and get something that will really make us sick. I've had enough of this watered-down brew."

They walked through crimson twilight past lethargic fat Indians to Cantina Row. Overfleshed, underdressed girls sat on the porch of Fat Annie's, swinging gartered legs and yelling raucously. The lamps had come on. In various cantinas several pianos and guitars played, mingling in the street in painful cacophony. Soldiers and teamsters and drifters and shopkeepers made an unsteady crisscross flow of traffic through the settlement. Ben Hannibal said, "I wish I were drunk."

"Better eat supper first."

"That'd just make it harder to get drunk."

"Why do you want to get drunk?"

Ben Hannibal thought about it. They passed Madam Lil's and a girl called out; Ben Hannibal waved at the girl without even looking at her. Finally he said, "I haven't got any reason not to get drunk."

"All right," Justin Harris said.

Ben Hannibal glanced at him sharply. "You're laughing at me. A fool kid trying to act like a wise and dreary old campaigner. Is that what you think?"

"Not exactly, but close."

"Well, then, you're probably right. This will do." Hannibal turned sharply on his heel into the Homestead Saloon—HONEST TABLES—WHISKEY—DANCING GIRLS. Ben Hannibal hesitated in the doorway and made a sardonic flourish. "After you, my captain."

"The worst place in town. I hope you're not carrying much money."

"Where would I get money?" Ben Hannibal said. "I'm one of Uncle Sam's finest. We don't need money, my uninformed friend. We're too good for it."

Going in was like threading a tunnel. The doorway was set in an adobe wall four feet thick. The ceiling hung low over a haze of tobacco smoke; colors were warm and dark; a half-visible pair of bartenders sweated along the length of the bar. Harris broke trail into the crowded, narrow room and found a place at a table. When he sat down, he saw that

Hannibal had stopped to talk with a thick-waisted girl near the door. Ben Hannibal shook his head impatiently and came away from the girl, who spat something after him in quick Spanish. Hannibal made room to sit down. "I'm glad I don't understand that damned language. All it's got is swear words. I'll buy." He left his seat to stand at the bar and order.

Three musicians plucked tentative sounds from their guitars and suddenly began to whack away in earnest. On the rear section of the rammed-earth floor men danced grimly with women who wore fixed, calculated smiles and expertly avoided plunging boots. Ben Hannibal returned to the table with two glasses and an unlabeled bottle. He took a drink and coughed tearfully. "Christ."

"Forty-rod," Justin Harris judged. "Maybe three weeks old. That's *aged* whiskey, Ben."

"If I were an Indian and somebody peddled me a gallon of this stuff, I'd jump the reservation, too." Ben Hannibal made a prune of his face and pushed the bottle away. "I wish I could dull my taste to the point where I could get up and dance with one of those cows. Hello, who's this?"

Harris had to turn in his chair and look over his shoulder. Through a channel between two men's heavy arms he had a glimpse of a slender dark girl at a card table.

"Georgia Bowen."

"Should that mean something to me?"

"Maybe not. She's no different from the rest of them."

Ben Hannibal said, "At least she's not wearing cowhide."

"She deals for a percentage of the house take, unless she's flush. Then she plays against the house. Sit down, Ben. She'll take your shirt."

"She can have my shirt," Ben Hannibal said. He was out of his chair. As an afterthought he picked up the bottle. "Come on—I want to sit in."

There were no empty seats at the girl's faro table. She had strong hands that peeled cards from the faro box like leaves of hard lettuce. Ben Hannibal stood behind a teamster and grinned. Georgia Bowen looked up. Ben Hannibal said, "Look at that hair, for God's sake." The girl's black hair cascaded loosely down.

Justin Harris said, "She spends an hour combing it that way." He didn't bother to lower his voice.

Georgia Bowen's eyes came around, and she stared at him with a quick, wicked smile. "Crusading, Justin?"

He answered her, "Scylla and Charybdis, Georgia. Just trying to keep my friend out of trouble."

"He looks old enough to get along without a mammy."

"That depends on who the mammy is," Ben Hannibal said recklessly.

Georgia Bowen glanced at two players. "You're having a bad run of luck, boys. Try another table."

The two men looked at each other and gave Hannibal an angry glance and left. Hannibal slid into the chair beside the girl, throwing his head back to drink from the mouth of his bottle. Justin Harris took the chair beyond. Georgia Bowen said, "The bet is seven."

Ben Hannibal found a coin in a pocket and laid it out. "Go ahead," he said. He was a little drunk and pretending to be drunker. "You've got the only human face I've seen in this town. Beautiful."

She gave him a mock-sweet smile. Harris watched, saying nothing. Georgia Bowen said, "Better tell your friend to put his money away, Justin. Tell him how I cheat at cards."

"To tell the truth, I don't care much about cards," Ben Hannibal suggested.

"Then you're at the wrong table, honey."

Ben Hannibal passed the bottle to Harris without looking. "When do you finish your shift here?"

"Whenever I like," she said. She had large dark eyes; they appeared black in the poor light. They swung around toward Justin Harris. "Why did you let him come in here, Justin? He's too damned innocent. But you always mind your own business, don't you?" She dealt the cards. "Go away and amuse yourself, then. I'm quitting after this deck." Her attention slid back to Ben Hannibal, who sat with guarded eyes, drinking, watching her hungrily. Justin Harris left his chair and went outside.

He lifted his boot to the porch rail and batted dust from it with a bandanna, which he then returned to his pocket.

He glanced at the surgeon's office, but there was no profit in the dusty walk over there. The adjutant was still confined to his infirmary bed, and walking across the parade ground to badger the surgeon wouldn't change that. Behind Harris were the sounds of rustling papers on the corporal's desk; next door, on the major's porch, Sergeant Major McCracken waddled outside to take a drink from the *olla*. Harris spoke to him. "Hotter than yesterday."

"Sure, and it is."

"How long have you been behind a desk, McCracken?"

"Off and on, ten years maybe."

"I don't see how you take it."

McCracken said, "The captain's not enjoying being acting adjutant, hey?"

"The seat of my pants gets bored."

"Ain't got enough fat on your seat. Me, I'm better equipped."

"That may be the whole of it." Harris crossed the distance to the major's porch and drank from the *olla's* cup. "You've seen commanding officers come and go, McCracken. You're not happy right now. Is it anything I should know about?"

"Major Cole's a good officer," McCracken said cautiously.

"And you're thinking he's had a bad deal of the cards."

"He's in the middle of a God-forsaken campaign—and if you're wanting my judgment, it seems like a bad time to change field commanders. Bad for the men, bad for the campaign. Might stir up Togomasai some, too. But like you said, it happens all the time."

"Exactly." Justin Harris leaned on his tone.

"You don't let up, do you, Captain?"

"I'm trying to get something out of you. Tell me this —what do you know about Colonel Mallory?"

"Ever seen him?"

"No."

McCracken put on a professionally noncommittal face. "I served on a garrison with him one time when he was a captain. Not in his unit, though. Some years ago, you understand. I was across the post and can't say as I knew him. The word was he was tough, he was fair, he knew how to get a job done."

"By the book? Stiff? Brass-hat?"

"I couldn't tell you, Captain."

"It looks like a spit-and-polish command," Harris said. "That might be a good thing, and then again it might not."

"Yes, sir," McCracken agreed judiciously. "Anyhow, it won't be long before we find out, will it?" He took out his monumental pocket watch, clicked it open, and studied the Roman face. "Nine hours to midnight. Begins to appear maybe Colonel Mallory won't be getting here in time for his own deadline."

"Don't bet money on that," Justin Harris advised.

"No," McCracken said, and retired into the office.

A girl stood before a framed "A" tent in Suds Row. She didn't look sixteen; she had an arm lifted to shade her eyes and was looking toward the enlisted barracks of "C" Troop. What she expected to see was not evident; no one was in sight. Presently the girl turned to her washboard.

Ben Hannibal entered the adjutant's office at four and sat on the corner of Harris's desk. Harris said, "Another night on the town, Ben?"

"Anything else to do around here?"

"I sleep once in a while."

"Time enough for that when you get old," Hannibal said with a quick, tired grin. He pushed his hat back. One boot heel swung rhythmically against the side of the desk. "Every time I go out on patrol I have to make some God-damned decision or other. I'm always scared."

"Play by the book until you learn."

"Learn what?"

"There's a time to break every rule. But not until you know the rules by heart."

"I thought I knew them down to my socks when I graduated from the Point."

"Just stick to the book," Harris said. "Get tough when you have to, Ben."

"Maybe." Hannibal shifted his seat. "*Damn* that McClellan saddle. Justin, I keep asking Georgia about you. She snaps shut like a lobster claw every time I mention your name. What did you do to her?"

Harris shook his head. Ben Hannibal said, "You'd like to tell me to stay away from her, wouldn't you?"

"It's like the lady said. I mind my own business."

"Is that a hint, Justin?"

Harris said nothing, but it was not long before Ben Hannibal got up and left the office.

In a while Harris went outside again. The sun was lowering, and a cooler breeze came down from the mountains. A quarter of the way across the post, at the barracks of his own "C" Troop, he saw Trooper Van De Reuter's nondescript little mutt trotting toward the doorstep. Trooper Hoag arrived just then, a scowling husky soldier, and kicked the dog out of his way. The dog yelped, whipped back, curling about itself, issued half a dozen painful yaps, and attacked the trooper's ankle. Half inside the door, Trooper Hoag cursed and kicked at the dog, shaking it off. It rolled in the dust and howled at Hoag; it went after him again. Hoag was ready to stamp on the dog when Trooper Van De Reuter appeared in the doorway behind him and spoke quickly.

Hoag uttered a sharp obscenity and kicked at the little dog. The animal bounced in and out, barking, worrying Hoag, snapping. Van De Reuter, no more than half Hoag's size, reached out and spoke again. When Hoag ignored him, the little Dutchman climbed up on Hoag's back and locked both arms around Hoag's throat.

Justin Harris shouted at them. He dropped off the adjutant's porch and loped across the compound. Spectators appeared at the stable, the smithy shed, the barracks doors, quartermaster's porch, and the side door of the Mess. Harris reached the barracks, but the fight was over: Trooper Hoag lay in a state of flushed collapse against the barracks steps. Van De Reuter paid no more attention to Hoag than he might have to a swatted fly. He picked up the whimpering dog and began talking softly to it.

Justin Harris knelt by Hoag and peeled back one of the trooper's eyelids. Hoag grunted, stirred, and sucked in a ragged breath. "Jesus," he said.

"Are you all right?"

"Jesus." Hoag braced his arms, got both feet under him, and levered himself upright. With one hand cautiously extended to the wall, he rubbed his throat. He swayed slightly. Justin Harris said again, "All right, Hoag?"

"I guess so. Sir."

Harris turned. "What about the dog?"

"All right," said Van De Reuter, rolling his "r." The Dutchman had two passions: his dog and the proper pronunciation of his name, "Vahn De Royter."

"You'll both have to go on report. Hoag, don't kick any more dogs. And, Van De Reuter, next time you get in a fight, don't go for the man's Adam's apple. You might have killed him."

"I apologize, Captain," said Van De Reuter with formal linguistic discomfort. He coughed.

When Harris turned away, he heard Hoag talking in his high-pitched angry voice: "I didn't mean the God-damned pooch no harm, Van De Rooter. Sweet Jesus, you didn't have to take on like that."

If the Dutchman made any reply, Justin Harris didn't hear it. When he passed the major's office, he looked up, intending to go by, but Major Cole was on the porch beside the sergeant major—two stout soldiers. The major said, "What started that?"

"Hoag kicked the dog out of his way."

"He's never acted like that before."

"It's an edgy day," Harris said crankily. He added, "Sorry, sir."

"I know what kind of day it is," the major said. He was gruff and testy. "I wish Mallory would get here."

"The sergeant major's taking bets he won't get here on time."

Major Cole said, "I'll take that bet, McCracken."

"No, sir. The captain's just making jokes."

It was a long, slow afternoon. The breeze died, and the heat seemed to build again. After supper the sun made a bloody last splash, and the guard changed, and Justin Harris went by his company's barracks to look in. A few men sat polishing boots and making ready for an inspection which, they assumed, Col. Drew Mallory would call tomorrow as soon as he took command. It was eight, and then eight-thirty, and Mallory did not appear out of the desert. The temperature dropped sharply. In the barracks long, discomfited silences hung between bursts of explosive, querulous talk. Justin Harris stood unobtrusive in the doorway and saw, every minute or two, Trooper Jensen get up to look through a window into the dark. Each time Jensen spoke the same two words: "Not yet."

The troop sergeant tramped around the room examining clothing and equipment. Now and then he mouthed comments of dissatisfaction. His name was Bodeen; he was a huge, ungainly figure of a man. He had a look as though he had been hewn from a single block of monolithic stone. Bodeen came to the door and gave Harris a defiant look and went on about his prowling.

Trooper Hans Van De Reuter sat in the far corner on his cot, feeding scraps to his dog. It was a small black-and-brown animal of mixed heritage; it had large spaniel eyes that paid no more attention to the other soldiers than did Van De Reuter. The dog lived under its master's bunk and seldom strayed from there except at night, when it hunted, and during barracks inspections, when it waited behind the building until the inspecting officers moved on to the next barracks. Then the dog would come around the far end of the building and resume its place. When Van De Reuter went into the field with the troop he left the dog with a bosomy woman who lived in a shanty on Suds Row and called herself a laundress. If the dog had a name, no one had ever heard the Dutchman utter it.

Van De Reuter's face was pointed like a rodent's; in some ways he resembled the dog: small, fragile, unsociable. He was neat and silent and evidently sick in his lungs, although he never went to the surgeon's infirmary. He had no friends.

Justin Harris watched him finish feeding the dog. Van De Reuter came toward the door and snapped his fingers. The dog trotted on clicking feet across the room; the two of them came out and Van De Reuter saluted expressionlessly before disappearing. Justin Harris heard someone say, "Gives me the God-damned spooks. I wish he'd hurry up and die, him and the dog both."

Justin Harris stopped by his Spartan quarters long enough to change his boots and splash tepid water in his face, after which he walked unhurriedly to the sutler's store. A tableau met his eyes there, and he stood in shadow outside the open door. The sutler was behind the saloon bar wearing a half-pained expression of resignation; a group of soldiers stood before him at the bar. Trooper Hoag was among them, but the leader of this particular pack was Cpl. Boone Blockman. Boone Blockman slapped the bar and demanded beer. He seemed to need to surround himself with men who would respect his toughness. He was twenty pounds heavier than any of his chosen companions. His phrases were colored by obscenities; it was a habit of speech without which Boone Blockman could not communicate. All his friends watched him expectantly except Trooper Hoag, who looked into his empty mug, cracking his knuckles abstractedly.

Lt. Ben Hannibal stood at the far end of the bar by himself, drinking beer and reading a newspaper.

Boone Blockman said, "To hell with Col. Drew Mallory, and to hell with that puking Dutchman and his God-damned dog. Jesus, I'm going to miss Old King Cole, you know that? It ain't fair, the old man getting a boot in the puking ass. Hell with the army. Sutler, fill me up again."

The sutler put up a beer, and Boone Blockman downed half of it in a gulp. He belched and swatted foam from his lips. Under his exposed suspenders the shoulders bulged inside the bleached blue undershirt. The sutler said, "Your bar tab stands at three dollars, Corporal."

"Puke it."

The sutler was a red-cheeked storekeeper, middle-aged, in a dark suit that fitted badly. He made a point of corking the beer keg. Corporal Blockman said, "You got a puking head for figures, ain't you, sutler? You keep everybody's account on the tip of your God-damned tongue like that?"

"No."

"Just me? Listen, you think I don't pay my debts?"

"I've got no opinions, Corporal. You've been working this tab since before last payday. You could have paid up then."

Boone Blockman reached for the sutler's lapel. "You puking little clown."

"All right." The sutler's skin flushed in the lamplight. "All right. No more credit, Corporal, until you settle up."

Boone Blockman had his back to the door, and Justin Harris could not see his face. Blockman's shoulders expanded. "By God, that's just what I'll do, sutler. That's puking right what I'll do." He dragged the storekeeper belly-hard against the back bar. All it took was a flex of his arm. The sutler's hands lifted defensively.

At the other end of the bar Ben Hannibal was watching. He put down his newspaper. "Cut that out, Corporal."

Boone Blockman's head reared. "Anybody ask you, Lieutenant?"

"What do you want the guardhouse for, Corporal?"

Trooper Hoag said, "You monkeying with fire, Boone. Back away."

Blockman did not move. Ben Hannibal said, "Please take your hand away, Corporal. I won't ask it again."

Boone Blockman's head swiveled, and Justin Harris could see his lip curl back. "Lieutenant, one dark night, by God—"

Justin Harris said, "That's enough, Blockman." He walked forward between cluttered dry goods counters.

Boone Blockman released the sutler and turned. His face was as obscene as his tongue: he was all brows and jowls and blued cheeks, slurred and colored by a stubble like a dark mown lawn. He had obsidian eyes, but they were rarely visible; they were accessible only down long tunnels.

Justin Harris laid a loose curled hand palm down on the bar. "Big inspection tomorrow. I think you'd all be tending to your chores."

Blockman's lips pushed in and out. He struggled with thought. Justin Harris said, "Get out of here."

"Yes, sir," said Boone Blockman with reluctant subservience. He had one look at the sutler, as if to fix the man's image in grudging memory. He transferred the force of his glance to Ben Hannibal and walked past Harris without a word. The troopers trailed him, and Hoag, who was last, paused long enough to speak.

"Thanks, Captain. Good night."

"It's the major's last night. He doesn't need trouble."

"Yes, sir."

"Good night, Hoag."

Their retreating boot heels scuffed the earth outside. Ben

Hannibal folded his newspaper; the rattling sounded like flames. The sutler made a show of adjusting his coat and settling his shoulders. "Blockman had me scared. The strange thing is, he wasn't drunk. Usually he's dependable as long as he's sober."

Harris said, "Once Colonel Mallory settles in, they'll ease down. Draw me a beer."

"Sometimes I hate the lot of them. They're a mean bunch, cruel as children. Peacetime soldiers are always a ragtag bunch."

"This is a funny kind of peacetime," Justin Harris said.

The sutler acted as if he had not heard. "And what about your Col. Drew Mallory? Where's he this fine night?"

"He'll be along."

"What makes you sure of that?"

"I'm not sure of anything," Harris said.

"How many of the rumors about him are true?"

"I've never seen him. I don't know."

"I must say you don't let much of anything get under your skin, do you, Justin?"

"I mind my own business," Harris agreed, and turned his head. He looked down the bar at Ben Hannibal, frowning over his newspaper. Harris said, "You were too easy with him, Ben. There's a time to be tough."

The sutler said dryly, "Stick it out long enough and you'll learn all the fine points, Lieutenant."

Ben Hannibal brought his paper down the length of the bar and brooded, not at Harris but into neutral shadows. "I've never been much good at that sort of thing. Pulling rank always seems kind of artificial."

Justin Harris said, "That's what rank's for." He tasted the tepid sizzle of the beer.

"I guess we're all keyed up. I wish I knew more than I know. Everything in my head's come out of books."

The sutler said judiciously, "Everybody has his first assignment somewhere, son."

Ben Hannibal folded the newspaper into a careful, neat square and laid it down and thrust it away along the top of the bar. The sutler said, "You haven't heard a bullet go by your ear yet. That's all that's bothering you. You don't know whether you'll fight or run, and you haven't had a chance to find out."

"Maybe I'll be too scared to run and too numb to fight."

"Maybe," said Justin Harris.

"Every time I go out on patrol I get tight, wondering," Ben Hannibal said.

"And you haven't gotten in range of an Apache yet," the sutler said. "Well, then, you're lucky. A fight's a lot of things, but one thing it's not, and that's fun. Especially with an Indian."

Locked up in himself, Justin Harris finished his beer and went out to the porch, where he stopped hipshot in the cool dark with his head thrown back and his hands rammed into his waistband. He waited several minutes, and Ben Hannibal came out by him.

"I didn't mean to badger you this afternoon about Georgia. It's your business, yours and hers."

"That's all right."

"I want to know about her. Is that a bad sign? I keep wondering about that."

"You wonder about too much, Ben."

"She's no good in your book. All I know is she's not like anybody else. I haven't found an easy label for her. If I could, maybe I'd quit hanging around her. Sometimes I feel like a pet dog. The trouble is I've got questions, I'm full of questions, and her answers are different from anybody else's answers."

"She hasn't got any answers, Ben—she's just given up, that's all."

"I think you're wrong."

"All right," Justin Harris said mildly. He took a backward step to prop his shoulder blades against the wall. "As long as you keep asking questions, you'll be bound to listen to anybody's answers."

"Then the thing is to quit asking?"

"Maybe it is," Harris said.

"Don't you ever commit yourself?"

A loud hailing of voices ran through the night. Harris said, "That will be the new colonel."

"This ought to be interesting."

"We'll see." Harris saw a shadow move into the compound—Trooper Hans Van De Reuter, a solitary pedestrian, followed by the little dog. Van De Reuter disappeared beyond the gate. A horseman rode out of the desert leading a pack horse, coming in from an angle past the edge of town. He was riding without hurry. Harris saw lights bloom in opening doorways and man shadows then fill the doorways. Corporal Blockman and Trooper Hoag were together in a splash of lamplight. The calling died, and no one spoke. Harris thought, I think Hoag will be a good soldier—he's stupid enough for it—but he's got to learn a little, just like Ben. The young are too damned curious. And the sutler's right— we've got a ragtag bunch, and no new colonel will be making a drill team out of them. If the colonel's as stiff as they say he is, then he'll break. Maybe that's better. Cole was soft enough to bend, and so he hasn't done his job.

But none of it really touched Justin Harris; he did not care. He watched the straight-backed rider approach the gate with a campaign hat set squarely across a shadowed face.

## 3

Drew Mallory rode to the gate leading a pack horse. The roped pack was light and rightly distributed. He had left nothing behind; except for his person Mallory owned little. Passing under the gate arch, he read the faded wooden sign. It flapped slightly on its chains in the night wind; across it was painted in a crescent a legend hardly visible: FORT DRAGOON, ARIZONA TERR.—EST. 1871

His face hid under the hatbrim's shadow. He answered the sentry's challenge and rode onto the post. A fat sergeant

major came out of the dark and saluted. "This way, Colonel."
A trooper took the reins and lead rope from him. A group
stood knotted on a lamplit office veranda. Mallory swept
them with a glance and took their formal salutes before he
stepped into the light. He was looking at Captain Mueller,
the adjutant; a nervous smile flitted across Mueller's mouth.

Major Cole said, "Welcome to Dragoon, Colonel."

The major's strictly calm face displayed nothing; Mallory
thought that from Major Cole's point of view it was a hell
of a thing to have to say as a greeting; the abdicating king
should not have to welcome his dispossessor.

Mallory inclined his head and climbed onto the porch.
His smoky eyes moved precisely from face to face; he knew
he gave the impression that he was engraving every set of
features indelibly on the slate of his memory. In the yellow
wash of light his face stood out strong and raw, etched with
sharp vertical crevices that set off his cruel mouth. His uniform was neatly creased and appeared as though he had just
put it on.

He locked glances once again with Captain Mueller.
Mueller spoke in a murmur. "Colonel."

The tone was deferential and the eyes unsteady. Major
Cole distracted Mallory. "Let's go inside, and I'll make intro-
ductions."

Mallory entered the office. The small group of officers followed, ranged themselves around the room, and watched
him from various angles and poses of uncertain expectancy.
Mallory doffed his hat, and his stiff white hair made a
metallic shine. His face was young enough, and he was as
lean as any man in the room, but not at all angular; the calculated revelation of his frosty hair rocked some of them.

He stood at one end of the room, making himself the center of it. Major Cole said, "My adjutant, John Mueller. He
shouldn't be here tonight—the surgeon didn't want to let him
out of the hospital."

The surgeon said in a gruff tone, "He'll live, I suppose."

Drew Mallory said, "You look fit enough, John."

"Thanks," said Mueller. "The doctor's an old woman."
But he did not smile.

Major Cole said, "I wasn't aware you two were acquainted."

Mueller's tongue threaded his lips and retreated. "We served together at Jefferson Barracks." He was gray and sturdy, not fat, but there was a thick roll of flesh at the back of his neck, folded there in a manner common to some Negroes and some Prussians and some Turks. There was a catalogue in Drew Mallory's head that stood apart from the rest of him, and as he looked at Captain Mueller, his catalogue registered: Mueller was fifty-one and could not expect a promotion before retirement; he had a competence for administration, and he had dependability, but he had no imagination. Drew Mallory had the ability to disregard the personal past.

Major Cole spoke each officer's name with slow care. As he gave each man his quick, firm handshake, Mallory fitted the men into his catalogue. He was not sure of one or two of them and reserved judgment. He met Captain Harris, "C" Troop. The captain was easy and loose, lantern-jawed, probably well-liked by his men, but Harris had a withdrawn and stubbornly unrevealing way of talking. Captaincy at the age of twenty-seven augured well either for Harris's military competence or for luck. In general, Drew Mallory distrusted careless, informal men, and he had the feeling that Harris had the great weakness of refusing to involve himself in any vitality outside himself.

He met one man, Lt. Will Sandin, who looked familiar and greeted him with bitter, bright eyes. The failure of his memory to place Lieutenant Sandin irritated Mallory mildly. He met Lt. Ben Hannibal, who had bones on which one day a powerful chunky body would hang, and he saw Ben Hannibal's face—sensible but clouded by uncertainty.

Pete Rubio, Chief of Scouts, ambled in and took Mallory's handshake without a word and faded casually into a corner. The half-breed's face was ungiving, broad with slit eyes set wide apart, brown as the earth.

The others—troop leaders, quartermaster, surgeon—fit easily into the catalogue.

This is the regimental backbone, Mallory thought, and now I'm its skull. The officers in this room are vertebrae in a skeleton boned with sergeants, corporals, troopers, horses, arms, equipment, all of it fleshed out by discipline and goal. One weak disk in a backbone can wreck a body.

Mallory studied them with care. When he spoke, there was no sign of whether or not he liked what he saw. He slipped a hand inside his blouse, withdrew a flat-folded document, and dropped it on the sergeant major's desk.

"These are my orders. You're welcome to inspect them." He directed his words at no one in particular; he saw Major Cole's flesh darken with color.

Drew Mallory spoke with half his mind, like a boy reciting a speech; he was watching them all. "On the twenty-seventh of April a Mimbreño Apache shaman named Togomasai jumped the San Cristobal Reservation with forty-six men, or warriors if you want. That was five months ago. Major, interrupt me if my facts are incorrect."

And don't look at me as though I'd betrayed you, he thought without heat. He said, "During the five months Togomasai has attracted several bands of followers, two hundred men or so, from among disgruntled Indians on three or four reservations in Arizona and New Mexico. They've built rancherias in the Sierra Grande about eighty miles south of the Mexican boundary, which they use as a base for horse-stealing and white-killing raids into the Gadsden Purchase area where we are now. You've attempted to reason with them and settle their grievances peacefully, but you've failed. No one can sign a treaty with them because they're not even recognized as a tribe by the Apaches themselves. The last officer to take them an offer went to them under a white flag and was immediately killed.

"In May the Twenty-sixth went into the field. In five months' time this regiment's campaign has inflicted minimal casualties—a dozen dead, perhaps thirty wounded. At the same time Togomasai has recruited a large force. The regiment has lost a captain, a warrant officer, two noncommissioned officers, and eleven troopers, each of them trained, fed, and equipped at government expense. Twenty-four civilians are dead or missing. I have a file listing the livestock and property that the Togomasai band has stolen or destroyed. It includes thirty-two army horses and eight army mules."

He thought, numbers mean nothing at all, but we have to use them. People can't think without them. Twenty-four civilians—the files don't care who they were, and neither do I, but you ought to. Maybe you knew some of them.

He said. "The Twenty-sixth has wasted five months. It's beside the point to fix blame for it, but I propose to change that state of affairs."

Their faces had closed up tightly like doors. He had antagonized them, and that was good; he had meant to. Major Cole was looking at him like a brave aristocrat at his executioner.

Mallory said, "I'll want the regiment to stand barracks inspection at reveille and full mounted inspection forty minutes after breakfast. At nine o'clock there will be a meeting of all officers, to include troop commanders and the Chief of Scouts, in this office. That's all, gentlemen."

He had not said he was glad to meet any of them or happy to be here. He had dispensed with formal frivolities and warmth, and he could see that they all knew he had done it purposefully. The officers filed out of the room, and in time Drew Mallory stood in the room with the major. Three or four lamps burned; the top of the sergeant major's desk was clean except for Mallory's orders. The room stood cool for an interval until Major Cole said; "I won't apologize or make excuses for the regiment."

"I don't expect it."

"I'd like to advise you of the particular problems you'll have here. The main issue, of course, is those base-camps of Togomasai's, out of reach in Mexico. But you'll have other difficulties besides that. The enemy's tactics make it impossible to anticipate his raids. You can't set traps. He's not fighting to hold any particular piece of ground—if he were, we'd have it much easier. If you asked me what Togomasai's exact purpose is, I couldn't answer you."

"He's angry, Major."

"It's more than that and more than revenge, I think. It's pride, too. I give him credit—he's a fine soldier, a worthy enemy. You'll find it frustrating to fight him with an army encumbered by wagons, saddles, the lot. We're not idiots down here, and we've been doing our best."

Mallory said, "Don't take that tone with me."

"I'm sorry. Your presence here is an insult to me. We all know it." The major took a long breath. "Let's go back in my office."

Major Cole turned into the private office and suffered an awkward moment until Mallory said, "It's still your office. Sit down—I prefer to stand. I've been thirty-six hours on horseback. A train wreck delayed me at Mesilla."

"Sorry to hear that. Anyone hurt?"

"The fireman broke his collarbone, a few people were bruised. A rail had been removed from the roadbed. Apache work, apparently."

The major sat. "You don't show your fatigue, sir."

"It's not part of my job," Mallory answered, but he saw that the major did not understand that.

A sense of regret appeared to touch the major briefly. "It's a poor desk, I suppose, but you become attached to insignificant things." When there was no reply, the major roused himself from his reflections and became brisk. "The official ceremony for the change of command—I've arranged it tentatively for tomorrow at one in the afternoon, subject to your approval."

"Satisfactory."

"Of course you're in the command from midnight on. I've sent my belongings to a spare cabin in BOQ—you'll be able to move right into your house."

"That wasn't necessary," Drew Mallory said abstractedly. "I don't pay much attention to comforts. It was kind of you."

"I have a Mexican housekeeper who'll come in to clean and cook if you wish, at eight dollars a month—unless you want to make other arrangements. You're not married?"

"No."

"My wife died seven years ago this fall. She was a good campaigner. My son's serving with the Sixth at Fort Grant." The Major's voice trailed off against the cool lifelessness of its reception. He cleared his throat lamely and made another attempt.

"You may not like Mrs. Loma's cooking. It runs on the spicy side."

"I don't mind. I'd just as soon eat in the Officer's Mess. Don't trouble yourself about it, Major—I'll make my own arrangements."

"As you wish. The records are organized for your examination. I can't say you'll like the job, but you've got a good group of men to work with. You can count on your officers. Of course, it will take time to accustom yourself to the regiment and the peculiarities of the campaign. If I can help smooth it out for you by answering any questions, I'll be more than happy to."

"I have no questions."

"I see. Well, then, you'll find the regimental files in those cabinets there. I'll see you at morning inspection." The major stood up, his face closed by the awareness that he had been rebuffed. "Good night, Colonel."

"Good night."

The major saluted carefully. When Mallory answered in kind, Major Cole went out and stood on the parade ground watching the dust stir in a cool wind, the ghosts of Twenty-sixth Cavalry troopers. There was a brief, quiet run of talk somewhere across the compound. Pete Rubio appeared from between two dark buildings. The major stirred and saw Rubio's hatbrim rise, indicating the scout's attention. Rubio came to him and said, "Good luck to you, Major," and went away. The major smelled the air, kicked the ground, and turned a full, slow circle on his heels. Presently he walked to his room.

A light burned in the window, although he had not left one lit. He pushed the door open and saw the sergeant major in the parlor.

"Well, hello, McCracken."

McCracken, discomfited, shifted his formidable weight. After a stretch of time he thrust a white wrapped parcel forward and worked his mouth into a tumbling rush of words that the major could not make out. The major took the parcel. "This is very kind," he said.

"Hell, Major, you know—"

"Never mind. It's done with, McCracken."

"Yes, sir."

"I won't forget any of you, either," Major Cole said.

McCracken formed a loose fist and straightened up and

stood that way, full of incoherent energy. A small spiral of
sour heat moved up from the major's belly into his throat. He
untied the package neatly and laid the wrapping aside. The box
was heavy, made of walnut. He lifted the lid. Inside was a Rem-
ington revolver, sleek and dark. On the wooden grip was im-
bedded a silver medallion engraved in tiny script:

WARNER COLE — MAJOR — 26th U.S. CAVALRY
FROM THE
OFFICERS AND ENLISTED MEN OF THE REGIMENT
SEPT. 1879

The plush box was lined with red felt. His initials were
engraved on the lid.

The muscles of his stomach tightened. "I'm grateful, Mc-
Cracken."

"Yes, sir." McCracken closed his fist.

"You look miserable." The major forced a laugh.

McCracken moved to the door and ducked outside. "Well,
good night, Major. Best of luck."

The major made no answer. In time the door closed.

In the headquarters office Drew Mallory had the file cabinet
open. His light burned into the morning, until at half past two
he extinguished it and walked outside. He crossed the
quadrangle past the darkened barracks, spoke to a sentry, and
made a circuit of the post until he reached Officers' Row and
found a small house with a fresh sign on the fence: *Col. D. E.
Mallory*. He brushed dust off the inch-wide top of the sign and
rubbed his finger, opened the picket gate and walked up the
gravel path between two precious strips of mown lawn. The
smell of fresh-cut grass was sweet and thick. From the dark
porch he could see the squatter town beyond "A" Troop barracks. The bell tower of a Spanish church stood black, and
beyond it the heavier mass and teeth of the Sangre range. In the
patternless litter of huts in town a few windows were yellow
with lamplight; the fort was still; he could hear voices and a
guitar coming from a cantina. The air, hanging above the
desert, was cool and very dry. He thought, soon it'll be October.
I wonder how early fall comes. He had never served in Arizona
before. He knew the West Texas heat, but perhaps that was
not the same.

He caught a motion with the corner of his eye. Someone stirred on the porch of the house next door. Aprroaching the edge of the porch, the movement became a woman. She stood in hazy outline with a shawl over her hair; she went back into the shadows and reentered the light farther away, going out from the house along the walk. It was three in the morning; Mallory's curiosity was aroused.

The woman went through the fence, came along the white picketting, and turned in at Mallory's gate. Lifting her skirts, she came up the three steps and threw her head back. "Drew? Drew?"

"It's late," he said.

"I used to keep later hours than this."

"You were young then, Beth."

"My God, do I look as old as you do?"

"I can't tell. Come inside where I can see you."

The door was not locked. He went in and struck a match, seeking a lamp. The room was small and clean. During the day it would be oppressively hot. He turned up a lampwick, lifted the chimney, bent to put the match to the wick. The woman said, "I'd better draw the curtains," and went around to secure the room. She was tall; her hair was down, long and brown. Mallory turned the lamp down to a glow and took a chair. When he sat, all his muscles loosened.

She drew her wrap around her. "I'm not at my best at this time of the morning."

"Never mind, Beth."

"I waited up for you. John went to sleep. He sleeps like a rock. Nothing will get him up before the bugle. God, I must look awful to you."

"No."

"I guess I don't have to fool you, do I?" She sat down, facing him. "I heard they were posting you here. You never wrote."

"What good are letters?"

"I was going to move to California."

"Alone?"

She didn't answer the question; she said, "I'd be gone now if I hadn't heard you were coming."

"Don't ever wait for a man, Mrs. Mueller."

"That's all I've ever done." She tipped her head far for-

ward to free her hair from the shawl around her shoulders.
"It was cruel to call me that. Are you still bitter?"

"No. I had to remind myself exactly who you are."

"As if you'd forgotten."

"As if I'd wanted to forget," he confessed with a shaded
smile. "You don't forget someone you've loved."

"You put that in the past tense."

"On purpose," he said.

"Still hard. The rock, Old Man Mallory. They've already
adopted all the same names for you around here."

"Have they?" He spoke as if he did not care. "I wonder if
there's any coffee in this place."

"You do look worn out. Though I'm probably the only one
who'd see the signs. Or is there someone else now?"

"No one else."

"I'm flattered." She left the room. There was a small
glow from the lighting of the stove. Drew Mallory traced a
crack in the chair arm with the point of his finger. The brisk
false mockery of her last two words hung in his mind, and he
remembered her as she had been—a part of himself.

She returned and stood, arms folded and shoulder against
the doorway. "This is a bad house. I had our own rebuilt by
Mexican laborers. I suppose I had to have something to do with
my little inheritance. I had it built of brick, because I hate
this adobe—I hate mud. I have a full-time gardener. Roses all
along the fence—you'll see it tomorrow. We soak the lawn
twice a day in summer. In a little while those young cottonwoods will shade the whole house, but I doubt I'll be here to
indoor plumbing and an icehouse underground."

"Admirable," he said.

"Oh, look, Drew, I know you don't care about these things,
but you don't have to be sarcastic."

He made a gesture. "Wherever you go, you carry it all on
your back. You're not a turtle—I'd think it would get heavy."

"Everybody has some kind of protection. A turtle's shell or
whatever you want to call it. Let's not talk about it."

"At any rate, it makes your husband comfortable."

"I didn't do it for him."

He turned up the lamp for a moment. The light reached out
to her. She had fine bones and no loose skin, but she showed her

age, which was the same as his—thirty-seven. Her face was molded in the shape of a shield. Long waves of her hair fell about the shoulders of her shawl. "Turn it down now," she said, and Mallory lowered the wick.

He said, "And now you'll go to California without your husband."

"Maybe. I don't like the desert. The coffee should be ready." She went out to get it. When she brought his cup to him, she said, "Your hair's gone all white."

"Runs in my family."

"I believe that's the first time I've ever heard you mention your family. I always thought you might have sprung full-grown from Zeus's head." She sat down, blew across her coffee, and watched him over the cup. "John has been ill."

"I know. He came to the meeting tonight," he said drowsily.

"He didn't tell me. I suppose that's like him. I can never predict what he'll do. Right now he resents his life—he resents me, he resents everything. He doesn't talk to me. Being laid up gave him time to think, and now he wants action again—he's tired of desk work."

"He was never particularly good in action," he said. "He belongs at a desk. He looked at me tonight as if he knew about you and me."

"He probably knew about us at the time. It was so long ago, wasn't it, Drew? He never said anything about it then. I suppose he had no proof—John's a careful man. But I think he knew all the time."

"And he still remembers."

"It's not the kind of thing you'd forget, is it? I doubt any man likes being reminded that he was cuckolded."

"The way you say that," he said, "makes you sound cruel."

"I'm tired. That makes a woman cruel. John and I have nothing, anyway—we treat each other like a pair of stones. That's real cruelty, Drew, if you want to see it. Days go by when we don't have a word to say to each other. That's why I want to move to California. But now—"She trailed off, stirring her coffee; when she looked up, his eyes were closed; he was asleep. She sat for a long while, watching his face.

# 4

Ben Hannibal sat with both arms stretched along the table, slumped over his drink. Justin Harris watched him dispassionately and said, "There are no heroes except fools and crazy men, Ben."

"You're wrong."

"All right, I'm wrong."

"I took one look at that white-topped colonel of ours and knew I'd never be that kind of soldier in two hundred years."

"In two hundred years," Justin Harris said, "we'll all be dead and forgotten."

"But in the meantime I'm wearing a uniform, and that's supposed to mean something. And I'm scared down to the seat of my pants. And so I get drunk. I sit here drunk looking at you sober, and I don't understand that, either—you've matched me drink for drink."

"I didn't want to get drunk. And I've had a little more practice than you've had. You're too young and too damned serious, Ben. And you've got to get up bright-eyed and stand in front of your troop in two hours. Better get to bed."

Ben Hannibal groaned—a young man in torment. The cantina was deserted; the two of them were the only customers; the barkeep yawned in boredom and stared at the clock, and back in a dim corner the Mexican was folded over his guitar, limp and half asleep, playing very slowly in melancholy strums. Ben Hannibal was showing no inclination to leave, and so Justin Harris pushed his chair back with a tolerant expression and propped his long bony legs, crossed at the ankles, up on the rim of the table. He hooked one arm over the back of his chair and smoked and listened to the soporific cadence of the guitar. He felt dulled to the point where he did not care whether he got any sleep or not, and he liked the guitar. It spoke sadly of the whims and pretenses of men; it worked its way inside him as few things did.

Georgia Bowen came and blinked against the lights. "I just finished a forty-eight-hour game and I want to drink," she said, She had tiny breasts, but her hips were round, and her face, not pretty, was narrow with a kind of clever warmth.

It occurred to Harris that she was a good deal older than Ben Hannibal. Harris said, "You had a winning streak."

"How did you know?"

"When you lose, you drink alone. When you win, you always want company to get drunk with."

"It's all the same," she said. "The important thing's the getting drunk. Robles, I'll take tequila."

"*Sí.*" The barkeep yawned and rummaged behind the bar.

Ben Hannibal was watching Georgia. His eyes never left her. His hand groped in his pocket, but Justin Harris said, "No, she's just won a big stake. Let the lady pay."

"Thank you," said Georgia Bowen. "You haven't called me a lady in a long time, Justin."

"A slip of the tongue. I'm too tired to remember my manners."

"In that case you're forgiven," she said. She sat down with her body tilted to one side; her elbow rested on Ben Hannibal's shoulder, and she picked absently at the hair around his ear.

Hannibal shook his head. "I'm ticklish."

"I know," she said; she was smiling at Harris.

Harris dropped his feet to the floor. "I think I'll go home."

"Wait a bit," Georgia Bowen said. "I'm buying the drinks, remember?"

"I've had enough."

"The hell you have. You're sober as a preacher."

"And pious as one," Ben Hannibal said.

"Oh," Georgia Bowen murmured, "I don't think you could say that about Justin. Not Justin. He's too careful to be pious."

The barkeep put a bottle on the table and spoke in grumpy Spanish. Georgia Bowen answered without looking up at him. "All right, go home, Robles. I'll lock up for you." When the barkeep was gone, she grinned. "He's got an anxious wife at home."

Ben Hannibal said, "Anxious for what?"

"Robles has eight kids. I suppose she's anxious to make it nine. But let's not talk about children. Justin hates them."

Ben Hannibal said, "I didn't know he hated anything."

"He hides his passions," Georgia Bowen said, quietly watching Harris.

He crushed out his cigarette stub under a boot sole. Georgia Bowen walked over to the guitar player and spoke to him. When she returned, she took a long drink from the bottle and turned, lifting both arms. "Dance with me, Ben."

Hannibal lurched out of his chair. Justin Harris made a motion, but the girl said, "Stay awhile," to him, and, unaccountably, he stayed. The guitar planed down a slide of chords in slow tempo, and Harris watched the chunky young lieutenant and the thin-boned woman dance under the low ceiling. Robles had left the door open, and the smoke haze was thinning out. The dancers circled near the table, and Georgia Bowen broke away long enough to take a drink; she danced away with the bottle balanced on top of Ben Hannibal's shoulder, and Harris sat without feeling, watching Hannibal's lips slide down her neck, seeing them dance with their bodies pressed together.

He did not have to think very hard about it to know that Georgia was using Ben Hannibal against him, and he wished he could feel more pity for the younger man. But Ben Hannibal's scars would heal, and in the end he would be wiser; it would not do to draw him away from the trough until he was slaked. Harris put his glance on the supple undulation of Georgia Bowen's hips and held it there until he heard her laugh at him. Half angry with himself, he held her eyes until she turned away, dancing. Ben Hannibal whooped and took the bottle from her, plugging it into his mouth like a cork and throwing his head back to drink. He was like that, swirling around in the dance with his head far back, when he lost his balance and tumbled to the floor with the girl. The bottle rolled away, leaking, and Georgia Bowen scrambled after it. She rescued it, laughing, and drank, on her knees.

Harris got out of his seat and knelt by Ben Hannibal. Georgia said, "Did he hit his head?"

"No. He's passed out."

"He'll have to learn to hold his whiskey better than that."

"What for?" he said. "He'd had enough before. He's got to stand inspection in an hour and a half."

"The poor boy."

She was standing up, looking down at him. "Well, then, you lug him home, and I'll close up the place for Robles."

He felt mildly heated. "Why don't you tell him the truth?"

"About what?"

"Tell him he's just a white chip in a no-limit game. Tell him he doesn't matter."

"Oh, Justin," she said. "He wouldn't want to hear that, now would he?"

Harris stood up. "Tell me something. What do *you* want to hear?"

"From him?" she asked. "Or from you?"

"Does it make a difference?"

"It might." She smiled. "Do you really care about him?"

"A little."

"Maybe it's just because I've held him up against you and you want to get me away from him."

"Make your own guesses," he said. "You'll have to find somebody else to get drunk with this morning."

"You'll do," she told him.

"No."

"You're so God-damned friendly, Justin." She walked to the back of the room and started putting out the lights. Harris felt the liquor in him when he picked Ben Hannibal off the floor and slung him across his shoulder like a grain sack. Georgia said, "I hope you get him sober in time for inspection."

"Do you?"

"Of course."

"I'm glad," he said dryly, and went out under his burden.

Outside he hesitated. It would not do to carry the lieutenant past the sentry. He had to get Ben Hannibal on his feet before they went on post. He turned toward the hotel, shifting the weight on his shoulder.

When he came out of the hotel half an hour later, he was steering Ben Hannibal by the elbow, but Hannibal was walking. He smelled like a coffeepot and looked like a corpse. Harris did not feel particularly jolly. Georgia Bowen met them as she came out of the cantina and latched the door. She smiled sweetly. "Good morning," she said.

Ben Hannibal stopped and blinked like an owl. He shook Harris's hand off his elbow. Georgia Bowen was going by when Ben Hannibal stopped her. "I want to know something. What's between you and Justin?"

She looked at Harris and waited a moment before she answered. "He decided I wasn't good enough for him," she said, and went away.

Ben Hannibal stared at Harris. "I'll be damned."

The surgeon almost forgot to answer McCracken's salute when he entered the headquarters office. With a grunt he turned all the way around and saluted. "You never saluted before, McCracken."

"I'm saluting now, Captain."

"I see." The surgeon turned around again. Mallory's door was closed, as usual, and the surgeon knocked.

"Who is it?"

"Captain Clayton."

"Come."

The surgeon went in and was walking forward when Mallory said, "Close the door, will you?"

When the surgeon sat down, he tucked his garrison cap under his arm and said, "Hot today."

"I thought it was moderate," Drew Mallory answered.

"The reason I mentioned it," the surgeon said, "you've got men doing double-time dismounted drill out there for extended periods of time. I've had two cases of heatstroke in the past ten days."

"I want them toughened up. It's October, and the heat should drop soon. Do you want to submit a formal complaint, Doctor?"

"No," the surgeon said. "Not yet."

Mallory showed a thin smile. His face was gaunt and powder-dry. "You're not afraid of me, are you?"

"Not particularly. I've served under a great many commanders."

"Your honest opinion, Captain. Do you think I'm over-working them?"

"I'd prefer to reserve my opinion. Obviously a few of them can't take it. But whether that's your fault or theirs, I'm not so certain. Perhaps some of them have gone too soft. On the other hand, there's such a thing as laying on too quickly with too heavy a hand."

Mallory said, "During the war I had command of a company that was shipped by sea from New York to New Orleans. We had to lie offshore because of naval conflicts, and the company was on board ship for three weeks. Quarters were cramped, and the ship was overcrowded. There was no room for exercise, and the entire company was in intolerably poor physical shape when we landed. These men ought to be able to march steadily day after day, with or without horses."

"On the desert?"

"If they have to. I didn't pick the field of battle, Captain."

"You're creating a strong resentment among the men. I expect you know that."

"Yes."

"On purpose. You want them angry—you want them to hate. Get them mad enough and they'll fight. Is that the idea? It's an old one. Sometimes it backfires—sometimes they'll betray you if they hate you too hard, Colonel. A little love helps sometimes."

"I don't want their love, Captain," Mallory said. "That isn't why I asked you to come here. I want your report on Captain Mueller's condition."

"Now or in writing?"

"Now. Verbally. How is he?"

"Completely recovered."

Mallory studied the physician's face. Captain Clayton was tall, totally bald, thin; he had supple hands and sharp, good-humored eyes. In the catalogue in Mallory's mind was the notation that the surgeon had served with distinction during the war—a war marked by medical butchery.

Mallory said, "To tell the truth, I'd hoped for something else."

"Why?"

"The adjutant's work is on post. He's doing a slipshod job of it."

"Because he wants action?"

"Yes."

The surgeon said, "I can't altogether blame him for that. Can you?"

"Yes."

"I suppose so," the surgeon said, reconsidering. "I suppose if I were in command, I'd have to blame him, too. You want me to give him the idea he's not well enough to go off campaigning."

"He might settle down if he had that idea."

The surgeon wiped sweat from his head. "You don't mind riding roughshod over your officers—I remember the tongue-lashing you gave Lieutenant Hannibal. But now suddenly you want to use subterfuge on your adjutant instead of direct action. Why?"

"It's not your job to question me, Captain."

"Of course," the surgeon said smoothly.

"Do what you can to discourage him."

"I'll try. Mueller's not easy to fool. Is that all?"

"That's all."

A lamp flickered on the colonel's porch; beneath it Justin Harris sat looking across the chessboard at Col. Drew Mallory. The dry night was turning cool. Harris pushed a pawn forward. The small yellow flame overhead made both men look gaunt and sallow. Harris packed his pipe and bent, cupping his hands to light it, then leaned forward, puffing, elbow on knee, watching the board with half-lidded eyes and spirits deadened by half a pint of whiskey drunk after dinner. Ben Hannibal had gone off with Georgia, and on his way home Harris had passed the colonel's gate and heeded the colonel's call: "Do you play chess, Captain?" Perhaps, he thought, he should have answered no. But he had nothing of interest to read in his quarters, and it was too early for sleep, and he had not felt like spending an hour alone with his thoughts. At times the one thing that could get under his skin was loneliness.

Mallory made a move and looked up, past Harris—Beth Mueller stood vague in the shadows on her own porch a few yards away. While Mallory watched, the woman turned slowly and went inside, and Harris had the familiar feeling that he was a spectator standing outside the window of other people's lives and yet not concerned in his own. Something stronger than acquaintance was between the colonel and the adjutant's lady, But, Harris thought, it is none of my business.

Mallory's white hair looked drab and yellowed. A fat man went by—Sergeant Major McCracken, bound for the sutler's beer tap. McCracken had the rolling, straddling walk of a sailor. He was Irish; he used his mouth and his fists and let everything else lapse.

Justin Harris said, "Your move."

Mallory pushed a pawn into the path of Harris's rook; in order to take the pawn, Harris had to advance his rook across two thirds the length of the board. Mallory moved another pawn, and, taking it out of play with his white bishop, Harris said mildly, "You've got only so many of those."

"They serve their purpose." Mallory moved his black bishop diagonally. Harris studied the board. Presently he pushed his white bishop to Mallory's back row, taking a knight, penetrating the lion's lair.

Mallory looked satisfied. "I'm afraid I led you into that, Captain." He moved his black bishop. "Check."

Harris said, "I was never good at this game." He moved his king a space, out of harm's way; Mallory castled and said again, "Check."

The king stood in jeopardy from both a rook and a bishop; he was against the base line. To the left was check by Mallory's queen; to the right were the hoofs of Mallory's knight, an L-shaped jump away. Only one haven remained—a diagonal advance toward the knight. Harris put his king there, and Mallory, unhurriedly shifting his second rook, said, "That's checkmate."

"Well done, Colonel."

Mallory had a cigar in one hand. He occasionally displayed one and toyed with it, rolling it from finger to finger. Harris had never seen him put one in his mouth.

"A few things you might learn from this," Mallory said. "If you plan a long-distance across-the-board checkmate with rooks and bishops and a queen along your own base line, you've got to have the middle of the field cleared. That's why I sacrificed a number of pawns. Pawns are buffers—you expend them tactically."

"Nicely put," Harris said dryly.

"You walked right in to take my knight, and that put your own bishop out of the way. What you had in mind was to take my men one by one until you'd gotten me outnumbered on the board. You expected to wear me down, and exhaust my strength. But positions count more than numbers in an offensive game. You might bear that in mind when you have a tactical situation in the field."

Harris paid scant attention to him. Mallory said, "Chess is strictly a soldier's game. I had a tactics professor at the Point who valued a good chess player over every sharpshooter and paper tactician in the class."

Harris's pipe had gone out; he searched for a match, found none, and finally stood up to light his pipe from the lampwick. "It could be a dangerous way to teach war. Soldiers aren't pawns."

"At times they have to be."

"Maybe. But not down here. This isn't a war—it's a stretched-out skirmish. There aren't any big movements."

Mallory said, "Any movement is big if it calls for a man to put his life on the line."

Harris thought, I guess that would depend on the man and whether or not he cared about his life. But he said nothing.

Mallory said. "The first thing an officer should know is that once you've committed yourself you've got to carry through all the way. There's no hanging back and no half measures. Either you fight or you don't fight. It's that clear-cut. Victory or surrender. Once the man at the top makes the decision to fight you fight with everything you have."

Harris was in a quiet mood, disinclined to carry the argument on. He made no answer, and Mallory said, "You don't care much about soldiering, do you? I'm surprised you've advanced so quickly. Was it luck?"

"I had a troop of the Fifth. We bottled up a bunch of Sioux near the Canada line and forced them to surrender after we'd cut them to pieces. I was noticed, so I got a captaincy. I suppose it was luck—that I happened to be assigned to that particular patrol on that particular day."

"Does it bother you?"

"What?"

"You said you cut them to pieces. Does it trouble you?"

"Not especially," Harris said. "They had to die of something. If we hadn't shot them, smallpox or old age would have done the job."

"You don't have many enthusiasms, Captain."

"I do my job, sir."

"But you're not likely to be a major."

"I suppose I'm not." Harris said good night and went away, wondering idly what kind of man lay behind Drew Mallory's constant military façade.

He was smoking on his back, fully dressed on top of the bed, with the lamp low, when someone knocked. He rolled to his feet and found a small boy at the door. *"El teniente quiere que Usted va, Señor."*

The child's grammar was bad, but Harris made it out. *"Adonde, Chico?"*

*"A la cantina del Robles."*

*"Tiene él salud?"*

The boy shrugged. *"Sí, creo."*

Harris found a coin and watched the boy race away. At a slower pace he went down past the gate and found his way through a reeking gamut of smells and shouts to the door of Robles's cantina. The church bells rang the hour—eleven or twelve; he didn't count and didn't know the time.

The cantina boiled with a crowd and gave off steamy sweat vapor. He did not see Ben Hannibal and became annoyed. Robles was in back of the bar, and Harris waited for him to swing down to the near end. When Robles saw him, his mouth formed an "ah" and he hurried down. "The *señor teniente* wishes you will come to the house of the *Señorita* Georgia."

"Thanks," he said crankily, and slithered outside like an eel through the sea of sweat.

Georgia Bowen had a place behind the stagecoach depot corrals. It was a poor hut: Georgia had better ways to spend her money. There was a single room, a bed, a little stove. Out back somewhere was a pump piped from a neighbor's well, and a squat-high outhouse. Basin and pitcher and half a dozen whiskey bottles stood on the single shelf beside a paper-covered window. The place was clean. Two of the bottles were full and a third half empty.

An empty key was a stool; Georgia sat on it. Justin Harris stood in the doorway, stooped under the top. "Where's Ben?"

"I haven't the slightest idea."

"Oh, for God's sake." He turned.

"You may as well come in," she said. "You came this far."

He thought of his dreary quarters and turned again, coming inside. "You knew I'd ignore a message from you. So you told them to tell me Ben wanted to see me."

"Some lies are harmless. It worked, didn't it?"

"All right," he said.

"You can help yourself to the whiskey."

He took down the open bottle and swallowed from it. He had left the door open coming in, and Georgia was looking that way, half amused. "You'd hate to soil your honor, wouldn't you, Captain?"

"There's no question of honor where whores are concerned."

"If that was meant to hurt, it missed, I'm afraid."

"What do you want?"

"I want to know if you really want me to leave Ben alone."

"Why?"

"I need to know if you care enough."

"About him?"

"About anything."

He waved the bottle around. "Do we have to bandy words around? Every time you talk you weave a crazy pattern. I haven't got the energy to play the game tonight. Say what you want to say and I'll go."

She went to the bed and lay back on one elbow, gesturing toward the abandoned keg. Harris stayed where he was. She said, "You were jaded when I met you. But there were some things you still cared about then."

"I've learned better."

She was angry: it showed suddenly. "You were worse than Ben, for God's sake! You found me with another man—all right, what did you think I was—a pristine virgin? I live the way I like. I have a right to—if I didn't want it that way, I'd never have come out here."

"It doesn't matter," he said. "Why bother to apologize to me?"

"Do you think I'm *apologizing?* For Christ's sake!"

He took a drink and watched her. He said, "I'm tired. Can I go home now, miss?"

"You can go to hell, Justin."

He grinned.

Georgia sat up. "Give me that." He had to walk to her to hand her the bottle, and she took a grip on his wrist, pulling him down; he resisted and pulled his wrist away. Whiskey splashed out of the bottle mouth. "Never mind," he said, and backed away; he set the bottle on its shelf.

"I'm not like you," she said. Her voice was harsh. "I don't give up when I don't get what I want."

"I haven't given up. I just don't want anything."

"You've cried yourself down to a puddle," she murmured. Her voice lifted unreasonably. "Why in hell don't you just kill yourself and get it over?"

"Are you asking me for a favor?" He felt his lip turn up crookedly; suddenly he disliked himself and felt imprisoned. He swung toward the door.

"Go ahead," she said, and that stopped him.

He went to the keg and sat on it. The rim of the keg dug into his buttocks. The crease was gone from his trousers at the knees; he hooded his eyes and looked at her and said, "If I worked at it, I might end up hating you."

"I wish you would."

"Too much trouble."

She said, "Ben was at my table tonight. Poker, not faro. He lost to a teamster. More than he could afford. He doesn't know enough about cards, and he wouldn't have played if it hadn't been my table. He went away drunk, and before he left he asked me to marry him. He can't handle me—he knows it—but he thinks he's got to lick every challenge that comes along, because he's not sure of himself and he's scared."

"If you're worried about him, why don't you leave him alone?"

"He'd only find somebody worse than me."

"Maybe," Harris said skeptically.

She walked to the shelf and picked up the bottle, but changed her mind and put it back. "Don't sit there like a scared cat, ready to jump if I move the wrong way. Oh, hell, Justin, you expected too much once and you were disappointed. Is that any reason to quit? For a change why don't you try living?"

"I've got no reason to."

"You've got no reason not to," she said. "Damn you, get the hell out of here. You disgust me."

He nodded his head and put his hands on his knees, got up and left. A feeling pecked at him, that he was missing something somewhere. There was something, not lost, but out of place.

# 5

It was just on sundown when Ben Hannibal's detachment trotted into the post. There was a creak of dusty saddle leather and the clank of canteens and metal gear. Ben Hannibal went up on the porch and noticed Sergeant Major McCracken's salute with half his attention. McCracken said, "Long ride, Lieutenant?"

"Too long." Hannibal was agitated. He went into Mallory's office to report.

"Close the door, Lieutenant."

Rattled, Ben Hannibal slammed it. Colonel Mallory said, "You're half a day late. I expected you at noon. 'A' Troop has already gone out, and I'd hoped to supply them with intelligence from your foray."

"I met them at the river," Ben Hannibal said, "sir. Gave them what information I had and sent my scout out with them."

"Your scout?"

"John-Ben Mingus."

"They have their own scout, if I'm not mistaken."

"Yes, sir. But Mingus knew just where to lead them. He volunteered."

Mallory's white hair glossed like feathers in a rainbow spray; he sat in sunset light from the window. "Your report, Lieutenant."

"Yes, sir. Mingus found some tracks yesterday. Unshod ponies, eight of them. Heading into the Huachuca country. That was more or less on the route of my patrol, and I decided to follow them. They went past Sonoita and up through Parker Canyon into the mountains. We got as far as Peacock Gap last night, never sighted any riders, but Mingus said they were only two hours ahead of us. I camped pretty far below the Gap. That's ambush country up there—too many places for an Indian to hide."

"And you turned back this morning?"

"Yes, sir."

"Why?"

Ben Hannibal looked drawn and cornered. "My orders were to run a routine three-day scout, sir. I had provisions for three days. As it was, I'd overextended the patrol by half a day."

"But you were in hot pursuit, or thought you were. Why did you camp instead of going on last night?"

"There was no moon. You can't see a thing in those mountains after dark, sir. All you see is big blocks of shadows. Anybody could be waiting for you. We'd have had to ride through Peacock Gap. There might have been five hundred Indians in there, for all I knew."

"You were frightened."

Ben Hannibal drew up straight. "I was prudent, sir. If I'd gone into an ambush, we'd have been chopped into hash."

"You turned your scout over to 'A' Troop. Now I suppose they're headed in the direction of Peacock Gap?"

"I suppose so, sir. They seemed anxious to pick up the trail."

"By now it's stone-cold. You ought to know how fast an Apache can travel. You've sent 'A' Troop on a useless errand, Lieutenant."

"I'm sorry, sir." Ben Hannibal held himself strictly. "I used my best judgment."

"It wasn't very good then, was it?" Mallory put a match to the desk lamp. The evening mess bell rang across the post. A breath of cooler air came through the window.

"According to my maps, Lieutenant, it's easy enough to drop

down into one side canyon or another and go around Peacock Gap. It might have lost you an hour's riding, but it would have done away with the danger of going through the Gap. You might even have picked up the trail on the far side and followed it into the Indian camp, surprised them and brought them down. But you didn't. You stopped and you made camp. You gave up a chance to take the enemy by surprise and engage him."

"I was obeying your orders, sir."

"On the first day here, when I took command, I made it clear I relied on every officer to use his head and his initiative when he was in the field alone."

"Yes, sir."

Mallory said abruptly, "Lieutenant, why did you camp instead of going on?"

"My men were worn out."

"I thought it might be something like that," Mallory said. His lips whitened momentarily. "Let me tell you something. Every decisive battle is won by men too tired or too scared. There's plenty of time to be concerned about your men, but when you're chasing or fighting an enemy you've got to forget that. In action a soldier is a tool, like a horse or a rifle. You care for your rifle in the barracks, Lieutenant, and you clean it when you can. But you don't stop in the midst of pursuit to oil it. Am I making myself understood?"

"Yes, sir."

"Dismissed."

Ben Hannibal's mouth was sewed shut. He stood up with slow care and saluted, made an about-face and left.

Drew Mallory went to the door. "Sergeant Major?"

"Sir?"

"Find the Chief of Scouts and send him to my office."

"Right now, sir?"

"Yes. Then you may go to supper."

"Yes, sir."

When McCracken was gone, the colonel went back to his desk and polished his boots. Someone knocked, and he put away the shoebrush and saddle soap unhurriedly before he spoke. Capt. Justin Harris entered the office and gave him a salute. "Saw your light and knew you were here."

Mallory said, "Business, Captain?"

"Permission to speak, sir?"

"About Lieutenant Hannibal?"

"Yes, sir."

Mallory tipped his chair back against the wall. He never appeared wholly relaxed; he was on guard. "It probably won't change anything."

"I know."

"Go ahead then." Mallory indicated a chair.

Harris sat. "He's young and a little green, Colonel. He'll get his boundaries laid out, and then he'll do all right. I'd appreciate it if you could see fit to give him a bit of loose rein for a while."

"I treated him quite gently, Captain, considering the blunder he made. It might have meant our first chance at a decisive engagement with Togomasai's men."

"Yes, sir. It wasn't cowardice that stopped him."

"Perhaps. He said his men were tired."

"They could have been my men," Justin Harris said, "or yours, Colonel."

"They're all mine. Most of all, Captain, they are mine." Mallory put his hands flat on the desk; his chair legs scraped. "For the sake of all of us, I'll assume you came here on your own initiative and the lieutenant didn't cry on your shoulder. Since he seems to be under your wing, I'd suggest you get his attitudes toughened up, and quickly. I don't mean to suffer another mistake of the same kind—and if one happens, Captain, I won't be as easy on him next time."

Mallory had a cigar in his fingers; he glanced at it and put it away. Abruptly he said, "What did you do to him?"

"What?"

"Ordinarily you don't seem to give a tinker's damn for anyone. You must have done something to Hannibal—what do you owe him, Captain?"

"Not a thing," Harris said. He left the office with a quiet salute.

Mallory puzzled it over. The Chief of Scouts wandered in with irreverent indolence and said, "You spend too much of the day working. Go fishing one day." Rubio picked up a chair and slid it back in a corner before he sat.

Mallory said, "Where would you find fish around here?"

"It ain't the fish that count, it's the fishing. Take a line down to the Smoke some morning. Maybe you catch a tadpole."

"At the moment I'm more anxious to catch Togomasai. Do you know where to find his headquarters in the Sierra?"

"More or less."

"Which is it?"

"I never seen his rancherias," Rubio said. "I know the country pretty good. You want them pinpointed, I can hire a couple good Yaqui scouts to go in there and plot them on the map for you."

"Do it."

"Sure," Pete Rubio said. "I'll need a little money to prod them Yaquis with." He seemed wholly at ease in the chair; his legs were sprawled out at improbable angles. "You figure to bust the Mex treaty?"

"No. But I want to know where I can find them. And one other thing—whose jurisdiction are they in down there?"

"Sonora Rurales, I reckon. But them Rurales don't want no part of Togomasai. You ain't going to talk them into doing your dirty linen."

"Who's the commanding officer?"

"Kominski. Colonel Vladislaw Kominski, heads up the northern Rurales. Lot of Mex I know be happier scalped by Apache than go through one of Kominski's jails. He's kind of tough to deal with. Hessian, I think they said he was, or maybe it was Russian—I forget."

Mallory said, "I want to talk to him. And I want to talk to Governor Pesquiera."

"You want to talk to God, too?" Rubio inquired.

"I'll meet them on any ground of their choosing. A border town should be satisfactory. Agua Prieta or Nogales. But it's got to be unofficial, and no one's to know of it."

"I'll see what can I do. Don't count on nothing."

"You'll do better than that," Mallory said gently. It made Rubio's eyes come up; there was just the beginning of a smile on his broad brown face, and Mallory knew he had the scout's respect.

Rubio stood up. "It'll take me a few days to find Yaquis I can trust, and maybe quite a while to put bees in the right Mex bonnets. You likely won't see me for three, four weeks."

Mallory filled out a piece of paper. "Give this to the paymaster in the morning."

Rubio read it laboriously. His lips moved. Afterward he said, "Get yourself a fishing pole," and went out, clapping his hat on.

The sutler's bar was deserted: it was late. Ben Hannibal stood footsore, rolling the beer mug between his palms and trying to decide whether to go into town or home to bed. The sutler was somewhere back in the room on a high stool, wearing spectacles, making entries in an account book. Delaying his decision, Ben Hannibal went around behind the bar and refilled his mug from the keg tap. He dropped a coin on the shelf and listened to it ring and rattle. His boots pinched.

Lt. Will Sandin walked into the room blinking; he had a nervous flutter, a habit of his eyelids. "Well, hello, Ben. Bearing up?"

"Sure."

"As long as you're back there, draw me a beer, will you?" Sandin tossed a coin, and Ben Hannibal was almost too sluggish to catch it. Sandin said, "I heard about the old man dragging you over the coals. The one-bars always get the heavy end, take it from me. Don't pay any attention to the old man." He had a New England voice, gone dry. Will Sandin was wiry and short. He carried a little billiard-round head with a thin haze of hair and a weight of drooping brown moustache. If he had been a foot taller, he might have been a dandy.

Ben Hannibal said, "How old are you, Will?"

"Thirty-six. I look closer to fifty, don't I?"

"I don't know. Promotions come slow, don't they?"

"The army's top-heavy with officers." Sandin accepted a mug of beer from Ben Hannibal and drank, almost daintily. "My last promotion was nine years ago. All the way up to first lieutenant. The pay's a little better, but I'm still bottom man on the totem. Next to you, that is."

"Why do you stick it out?"

"I'm a good soldier," Will Sandin said. "One day that will mean something."

"Will it?"

"Hell, and I thought *I* was sour."

"Forget it," Ben Hannibal said.

Sandin drank more quickly and put his mug down empty. "Some of them get promoted quick enough. Maybe you'll be one of the lucky ones. Look at the old man. The God-damned Rock. Mallory was brevetted major when he was twenty-one."

"That was in the war. And I don't give a hang for brevet ranks. They strip off like old wallpaper."

"Why, I never knew you were ambitious, Ben."

"I guess I'm not. Something to complain about, that's all."

"Mallory, now—there's real ambition, you know it? His hair turned white and the son-of-a-bitch got crotchety, but he's only thirty-seven. Thirty-seven, Jesus! Only a year older that I am. I graduated the Point in '63 when Mallory was at Vicksburg, and he'd only graduated six months before me. A damned long time ago, Ben—you'd have been about six or seven years old then. By the time I got my commission, Mallory was a God-damned brevet captain, permanent first lieutenant. In a war the ones lucky enough not to get shot are the ones who get promoted. I followed the bastard's career all the way, and I hated his stinking guts every time he took a battlefield promotion while I was stuck on the damned Potomac running school-boy errands for the puking War Department. Hell, he's got forty pounds on me, and I could have licked him any time in the past sixteen years. I still can. Him and any man in this regiment, except maybe Justin Harris and Sergeant Bodeen and that big ape in Harris's troop—what's his name?"

"Corporal Blockman?"

"That's the one. Corporal Boone Blockman. He was a bare-knuckle boxer once."

"How'd you find that out?"

"I like to talk to people. I get curious about them." Will Sandin's voice grated on a rough edge. He acted as though he bore a vast accumulation of resentments. "Mallory made his permanent captaincy before Appomattox. He was brevet light colonel then. He had the God-damned luck to be with Grant all the way through, the whole God-damned way. All he paid for it was a Minié-ball nick in his thigh. Christ, it's taken me all these years to get a line assignment. This is the first action duty station I've ever had. Sixteen useless years, Ben.

You're good and God-damned lucky to draw it first time out."

"Yeah," said Ben Hannibal.

The sutler walked by in baggy pants and stooped to put his ledger away under the counter. "I'm about to close up, gents."

"One more," Will Sandin said, "and we'll go home." He tossed a coin to the sutler. Ben Hannibal filled the mugs, corked the keg, came around the end of the back bar. He looked preoccupied.

Will Sandin drank. His thick lower lip appeared to pout beneath his moustache. He spoke suddenly in a rush.

"It's a damned unfair system, Ben, and you'd be better off out of it. Look at me—I'm better read than Mallory, I'm as fit as any man alive, I've got a head for figures and mechanics and tactics, my men don't resent me—in fact, I think some of them like me well enough—anyway, at least I get along with the people under me without making sparks. I keep a journal— did you know that? It's going to make damned interesting reading one day. Christ, Ben, I'm a good officer. There's not a thing wrong with me. But I'm a God-damned line lieutenant after sixteen years' service. Hell, Justin Harris has worked his way all the way to captain in less than half that time, and I'm a cleverer man than he'll ever hope to be. Then you take Mallory, and I defy anybody to figure him out. He's obsessed that everybody's got to follow the stinking book. To the letter. He doesn't even know that those God-damned Apaches haven't *read* the book. We've got to follow it page by page, but then the old man goes out on a wild hair and uses the riskiest and most unorthodox campaign tactics I've ever heard of. You ever hear about that march he led across the Staked Plains? If he hadn't had the devil's own luck, he'd be dead now, him and every man he had in that command. Jesus. He hasn't got a single friend in this regiment. But there he is on the number-one horse. I'll tell you the truth, I can't make it out. I never have. The system's no better than a roulette wheel. You'd be smart to resign while you're young enough to change."

Ben Hannibal said absently, "Time to go."

Sandin went out with him, talking earnestly. "Do it, Ben. For Christ's sake, get out while you can." When Hannibal made no answer, Will Sandin put his hands in his pockets and walked along round-shouldered, whiskers drooping.

Justin Harris led his patrol off the desert at noon, posted them to the stables, and climbed the colonel's porch. Sergeant Major McCracken did not salute, but only said, "The colonel ain't here."

"Sir."

"Sir," McCracken said with a pained look. "He went out to the Agency. Be back tonight. I guess you're to report to the adjutant, sir."

"That's customary," Harris agreed dryly. He stiffened his right hand and began to lift it slowly, giving McCracken plenty of time to whip up his own salute first. When Harris left, he heard McCracken's low curses.

Next door the adjutant's corporal came to attention and went into the adjutant's back office to announce Harris. Harris remembered to take his hat off. He moved into the back room and found Lt. Will Sandin there talking with the adjutant. Captain Mueller rubbed the back of his bull neck and tossed off a salute that was more of a wave. He had a distasteful look, as if he had just eaten something sour. "I suppose you've got bad news, too?"

"I haven't got any news at all," Harris said. "Three days around the Arrowheads and Arroyo Seco. No sign, no trouble, nothing."

"Be glad of that," Will Sandin said. "I just came in from a squad patrol up to Kitchen's ranch. A dozen Indians raided them yesterday and got away with eight horses and three mules."

"Anybody killed?"

"No. Kitchen's place is a fort." Sandin tugged his moustache points, one after the other. His eyes blinked rapidly. He was little and round-headed and looked like a librarian surprised by daylight. "I'll shake down my squad," he said vaguely, and left.

Captain Mueller said, "I wish I could warm up to Sandin."

"What difference does it make?" Justin Harris asked.

"I don't particularly enjoy disliking people. But I just don't like Sandin."

"It's not as if you had to sleep with him."

"People matter to me, I guess. They don't to you, do they?"

"Not very often," Harris said.

Mueller was scowling at the hairy back of his brawny hand on the desk. Mueller said, "You, for instance. You used to be pretty cheerful, but I haven't seen you laugh in a long time."

Harris said nothing. He felt like leaving but had no adequate excuse to do so. It was uncomfortable to look at Mueller; the adjutant was actively unhappy, not able to accept the idea that he was chained to his desk by duty. Harris wondered if Mueller knew about Colonel Mallory's interest in Mueller's wife. If there was such an interest. It was a speculation that drifted in and out of Harris's mind; he never had the energy or desire to find out if anything actually existed between Beth Mueller and Mallory.

Mueller said, "Dr. Clayton's been trying to tell me I'm too sick to ride a horse. He's lying. I wonder why. I suppose the colonel put him up to it, but it just doesn't make sense. You'd think the colonel would be happy to send me out on patrol."

"Why?"

Mueller hesitated. "We're shorthanded," he said lamely, and Harris knew that, after all, Mueller *did* know. After that it was hard to stay in the room with the man; Harris made a poor excuse and left. On the porch he thought, I'm too God-damned sensitive, and wondered how that could be.

He changed uniforms and put on a garrison cap, read a few pages in a catalogue and left his quarters, driven out by the room's solitary depression. He made a detour to avoid passing the front of Drew Mallory's house—he didn't want to be invited to play chess. When he reached the post gate, he realized that Mallory was away at the Reservation; it didn't matter.

It was warm, but summer heat was gone; November was eight days away. The dust was dry as ever. He moved restlessly in and out of the sutler's, down past the corrals and Indians. The cantinas were empty, most of them closed; it was lunch hour, and after that would come the siesta, and not until four or five o'clock would business pick up. Troopers stayed on post with their chores until after supper; the rest of the world worked, too. Harris did not feel like part of it. He had plenty of work of his own—paper work in troop administration—but he lacked the patience to face it.

Finally he walked into Georgia Bowen's shack without

knocking. His entry awakened her. She rolled her head on the pillow and looked at him sleepily. "Well," she said.

He took a bottle down from the shelf and took a sip from it. Not liking the taste, he put it back. Georgia Bowen said, "The light hurts my eyes. Close the damned door."

"Too gloomy in here. Let it stay open."

"Jesus," she said. She sat up, naked, pushing the rumpled sheet away. Her hair was knotted: she smoothed it back. He glanced at her without much change in expression. She said, "I still look pretty good for my age, don't I?"

"I suppose so."

"I'm twenty-eight," she said. "And I look it. Most of these hags out here look fifty by the time they reach my age."

"Maybe they are fifty."

"They die before they're thirty-five." She stood and faced him provocatively. He made a motion toward her but stopped. One side of her mouth lifted in a smile; she slipped a shirt over her head and found a pair of trousers above the bed. He watched her climb into them and button them up. She said, "I stay out of the sun—that's what keeps me alive. What keeps you alive, Justin?"

"Nothing in particular. One day comes after another, I guess."

"And you get lonelier all the time."

"I guess that's right," he said.

"You're too old to be a bachelor. You've turned cranky, like an old maid. Why don't you take any interest in things any more?"

"Maybe I got tired of turning over rocks just to see what would crawl out from underneath." He added, "I didn't mean that personally," in a very dry way.

She snapped at him, "Just what is it you think you're hiding, Justin? Or are you just hiding from yourself? Does it do you a lot of good to pretend you hate me?"

"What makes you so sure I'm pretending?"

"You came here just now," she said, and let the statement hang before him until its meaning reached his center.

Finally Justin Harris said, "That's something to think about." He was frowning. He turned without thinking, got the bottle down and began to drink from it; he sat down and hung his forearms over his knees, bending his head forward. He felt tired and uncertain, and suddenly he was afraid because he did not know the reason he had come here.

The alert corner of his mind shrank. He was vaguely aware of Georgia lighting a cigarette. When she drew on it, her cheeks sucked in strongly. She seemed nervous or excited, but she sat without moving, without talking. A pall of smoke rose from her face. Justin Harris kept drinking from the bottle until she said to him, "Cut that out. Do you want to show up drunk for evening report?"

"I don't care."

"Oh, for Christ's sake."

He took a pull at the bottle. Georgia Bowen exhaled a blast of smoke and walked to him; she dropped her burning cigarette down the mouth of the bottle. Justin Harris said, "What the devil did you do that for?"

"To keep you from making an ass out of yourself."

He looked at the cigarette, logged and brown, floating submerged inside the whiskey. With an inarticulate sound he flung the bottle from him and rammed toward the door, hearing the bottle crash.

She got before him and flung her arm across the doorway. "It was my whiskey, damn it. I can do what I want with my own whiskey, can't I? You barged in here without a by-your-leave, but you won't leave the same way, Justin."

He drew up short. "Get out of the way."

"No!" She lifted her head. "You can push me out of your way—if you care enough."

His eyes were round. He took a step toward her, raised his hands, and slowly turned the palms up, staring at his hands as though they were unfamiliar objects. Crosswind drew air out through the doorway, and he could smell the strength of the spilled whiskey. Beyond Georgia Bowen, beyond the shadow of the shack, the sun turned the earth cruel white. The brightness made it difficult to make out her face. He reached out like a blind man groping; he touched her on the shoulders and she stiffened like a piano string, with a quick indrawn breath. His hands laid their full weight on her. She said, "Justin?"

He dragged her tight against him and dropped his face to her shoulder. The cloth muffled his voice. "Don't ask me anything."

His hands brutally kneaded the flesh of her back. His mouth was open on her shoulder, and he felt her lips turn against his ear: he wanted never to move from this spot.

In the end she broke away from him and went across the room. He turned and stood awkwardly, gaunt, his eyes now bitterly alive.

She could have sat on the bed, but she chose the keg instead. "I'll have to clean up that mess now," she said bleakly. "Right now, or it will sink into the ground and stink for a week. I'll pour salt on it. Yes. And then mop it up. I hope I don't get cut picking up the broken glass." She looked at him, not expecting any apology, not expecting anything. She said, "I told you Ben Hannibal asked me to marry him."

He knew what she was going to say then. He said quickly, "He was drunk. You said he was drunk."

"He asked me again. Sober."

He didn't want to hear it, but he was afraid not to. He waited, gathering his composure. Georgia Bowen said, "I told Ben I'd marry him."

All he could think to say was, "You poor fool." And he went out scared, after all.

# 6

The orchestra, composed of regimental bandsmen, was a little stale, a little flat, a little out of tune. A fine covering of dust and the close residue of the heat of the day just past reminded the dancing officers and ladies of where they were. The long room smelled of soap and leather. Tables stood pushed against the walls. The orchestra stood, stiff and starched, on an improvised bandstand and flailed away at tunes from places far away.

Wih a frigid grin at the end of a waltz, Lt. Will Sandin went to the bandstand. He whispered in the bandleader's ear and walked away into the crowd. The bandleader spoke to his musicians, whereupon the orchestra broke into a martial "Garry Owen."

At the song's first bars, Col. Drew Mallory's head shot back and his eyes swept the room. Justin Harris, who had just entered, stood in the doorway smiling slightly; "Garry Owen" had been Custer's regimental theme, and everyone in the room knew what it meant. Ben Hannibal was at the punch bowl with Georgia Bowen, and Ben Hannibal alone seemed not to recognize what was happening; he had an absolutely tin ear and wouldn't have known a sonata from a march. Adjutant Mueller, at Mallory's shoulder, was watching the colonel, half afraid and expectant. A lieutenant talking to his wife stopped his mouth in mid-phrase and turned his head slowly, and Justin Harris saw a secret, pleased amusement on the face of Lt. Will Sandin.

Captain Mueller said, "I don't think that's very funny."

"No one's hurt by it," Mallory said surprisingly. He proceeded to ignore "Garry Owen," which the orchestra dutifully played through to its finish, thereafter squeezing into yet another limping waltz.

Harris went to the punch bowl and glanced at Georgia. She wore a dove-gray dress. A demure light sparkled in her eyes. Her presence was an affront to most of the ladies, and Georgia was fully aware of that. She tucked her hand in Ben Hannibal's elbow and cocked her head toward him possessively. Hannibal was flushed. Justin Harris pitied him. Georgia gave Harris a strange glance and led Ben Hannibal onto the dance floor, raising her arms to him. Harris reached for a cup of punch and hoped it was strong.

Drew Mallory moved around the room, talking to people, looking uncomfortable; he was not at ease with small talk. His dress uniform was precise and neat. His hat lay on a chair by the door, a cavalry-blue Kossuth hat with crossed sabers over the grade insignia at the front of the crown. Surrounding the two golden sabers was the white sunburst emblem of Sheridan's cavalry corps. It was a notable hat; it identified its owner exactly, in a military theater where the custom for commanding officers was eccentricity of uniform.

Ladies in gowns that hadn't been worn since last year at this time, or in gowns they had spent months making for this occasion, made whirls of color down the lengh of the room. Captain Mueller said to the colonel, "That tune wasn't the bandleader's idea. Somebody put him up to it. I can find out who it was."

"Never mind," said Mallory.

He watched Beth Mueller draw near; she nodded to him with cool reserve and spoke to her husband and swung with him onto the dance floor. The overriding music was a false note of cheer. Mallory stopped at the punch bowl and nodded to Justin Harris and filled his cup. Couples turned by like clockwork figures on a music box. Now and then Mallory had a glimpse of Mueller, the folded ridge of flesh at the back of his Prussian neck, Beth's fine-edged features half hidden by the mass of his shoulder. Mueller danced with grim stolidity, and Beth's expression seemed drawn. Once her eyes gripped Mallory's and held them until Mueller circled her around.

Justin Harris began to say something, and Mallory spoke an abrupt word to him, cutting the man off. Mallory went toward the door, picked up his hat, went outside. It was noticeably cooler in the dark outdoors. He stood on the Rec House stoop, breathing deeply, cursing silently.

He heard the waltz come to an end. Beth Mueller brought her husband outside and looked quickly at Mallory as if she were surprised to see him there. "I've been dying for fresh air."

"Starting to cool off now," Captain Mueller said. "It'll be fall soon."

"Fall," Beth said with a wry turn of mouth. "You need instruments to register it in this country. I wish I could see a forest turning color and smell the air."

Mallory kept his gaze fixed on the far end of the quadrangle. Captain Mueller turned squarely toward him. "A word with you, Colonel?"

Mallory brought his attention around. Mueller said, "Lieutenant Sandin's wife is about to give birth."

"I know."

"He ought to be here at the time. I'd like to take his troop out on Tuesday's patrol."

"This isn't the time or place." Mallory said. "We'll discuss it in my office, Captain."

"Thank you," Mueller said, and turned back inside, alone.

Beth said, "You've known him a long time, Drew. Can't you use his first name?"

"He came to me about military business."

"You need to unwind, don't you?" She moved closer to him. "They're a good lot, Drew. You treat them too strictly. They're far better than the officers you had at Jefferson. None of them are drunks or martinets."

"Then it's strange they haven't done better. There's not one of them with imagination. Maybe the desert gets inside them—they don't seem to care."

"You're wrong. You've got several bright men, but you keep them pinned down like butterflies."

He said nothing. There was a quiet run of moments; the orchestra began to play. She said, "Have you been watching Will Sandin?"

"Not particularly. He has a small man's arrogance."

"Don't you remember him from before?"

"I believe he was a year behind me at the Point. I don't remember ever talking to him then."

"He's still a lieutenant. It's given him a grudge against you. I heard him complain to John one evening."

"I suppose it's understandable," he said indifferently.

"Doesn't hatred bother you, Drew?"

His shoulders lifted. "It may be a challenge for him. I'll watch him—I watch everyone, this being the kind of world it is"

Ben Hannibal came out the door with Georgia Bowen on his arm. Seeing the colonel on the porch, Hannibal saluted stiffly and led the girl down to the far end of the porch and stood there, all but concealed in the darkness, talking to the girl. Beth Mueller said, "Strange about those two. I've heard they're going to be married."

"Maybe it will settle him down," Mallory said.

"He's so young, Drew. He hasn't decided yet what kind of soldier he wants to be."

"I know. He's been looking for an example to imitate, and he's made the mistake of latching onto Harris's coattails. Harris may have been a soldier once—it's hard to tell. He's just a shell now. He had a soft place in him somewhere, and I can't trust him."

"I think you're wrong," she said. "He's had some kind of trouble lately, but he's got a lot of good in him. I think your judgment's wrong, Drew. You'll be needing Justin—a star for the men to follow. They'll do what you want of them, but they'll never love you the way they will a man like Justin."

"I don't ask it of them."

She glanced toward the half-open door. Through it came a triangle of light and the music of the *varsovienne*. A small group of officers had gone out the side door and stood smoking by the corner of the building. Justin Harris's rawboned figure was easily recognizable in that group. Mallory said, "In spite of what you believe, Beth, there are times when even love is out of place."

"Are there? I can't think of any."

He made no direct answer; instead he said, "You're right in one thing. The regiment's wallowing in self-pity. It needs someone to set an example, a star to follow. But I don't think Harris is the man for it."

"Then who is? Are you?"

"No. I have no illusions about that."

"You have too few illusions, Drew," she said in a peculiar small voice. She turned one side of her body into the light; it gleamed on the green brocade of her gown. "Oh, Drew, it's been such a long time. Why do we have to draw a line and keep our talk on the cool and distant side of it? Can't we talk about ourselves? We had warmth between us—what happened to it? You used to talk of sweet things to me."

"I've lost the capacity," he said. "There isn't time for it any more."

"Then you're in too much of a hurry. I'm so sorry, Drew."

She went inside quickly. Mallory stood still, thinking of what they had said, thinking particularly of Justin Harris, who was just now laughing and clapping a lieutenant on the back. There had been something forced and false about Harris's gaiety the past few days, and Mallory wondered if it had anything to do with Ben Hannibal's announced engagement. Lately Harris had been too careless with his laughter, too hearty.

Ben Hannibal and his girl came back down the porch toward the door, and Mallory stopped them. "I've heard you two plan to be married."

"That's right," Hannibal said. "Have you met?" He introduced Mallory to Georgia Bowen. Mallory liked the woman instantly, but he saw immediately that she was too much for Ben Hannibal. He watched them go inside and wondered why it was so easy for a man to make a fool of himself at the whim of a woman. He thought, I suppose it takes a man a long time to grow a backbone of his own.

At the corner of the Rec House the group of officers raised their voices in laughter. Justin Harris turned and put his back to them, cupping his hands to light his pipe. His cap bill rose, and he stood looking up toward Mallory; the flare of the match glittered on the surfaces of his eyes. All the laughter drained out of his face; he shook out the match and with a bare nod of the head turned back to his companions.

The orchestra struck up a reel. Mallory stood in solitary half-darkness, felt the touch of cool air, and realized that Harris disliked him because of his single-minded, humorless sense of duty. In a strange way it encouraged Mallory; it was better than the indifference that Harris had shown up to now.

Mallory descended the porch steps and went around the end to the knot of officers. Their talk dropped off; all of them were silent, at bay, when he came among them. He said, "Sorry to disturb you, gentlemen. Captain Harris?" He walked away without waiting a reply, passing through the edge of the group. Faces turned toward him, closed like oak doors. He went as far as the central compound and halted in the shadow of the regimental mess, seeing a light in the window of the adjutant's office where the O. D. kept vigil. Footsteps crushed the earth, and when Mallory felt a weight behind him, he said, "How well do you speak Spanish?"

Harris was gaunt and wiry in the dark; he gave the impression of a man containing fierce energy under pressure. "Well enough to get along."

"Could you interpret at an official meeting?"

"Yes."

"I have an appointment Friday at the town of Lochiel with two Mexicans. I'd like you to accompany me with a small detail—about four or five men."

"All right," Justin Harris said without curiosity.

"Don't mention it to anybody," Mallory said. "When we leave here Thursday noon, you'll bring a suit of civilian clothes in your pack."

Harris was turning away when Mallory said, "Captain, you'll salute me at the end of an interview."

Harris came back around on the balls of his feet, slid them together, drew himself up, and slowly lifted his arm in precise salute. Mallory snapped an answer to it. He couldn't tell whether or not Harris was smiling. Harris performed an exact, deliberate about-face and marched away at attention, shoulders lifted. Music drifted down from the Rec House, and Mallory stood alone on the spot, watching the captain disappear.

On Sunday rain fell lightly most of the day. Men without chores stayed inside. The woodwork had a steamy odor, and troopers played cards and read books. For some of them the day had its recollections of distant rainy Sunday afternoons, the sky gray behind trees bent by the wind, or a puddled cobblestoned street traversed by enclosed carriages, street lamps doubled by their reflections in the water. Although the weather was inclement, Trooper Hans Van De Reuter walked his dog for an hour, as was his habit, and when he returned to the barracks, the Dutchman was coughing badly.

Monday broke cloudy but dry. The hard sun burned off the clouds by noon, and McCracken made many trips to the porch water jug outside his office. Ben Hannibal's troop went out on a foray with rations for three days. Cpl. Boone Blockman played a game of horseshoes with Troopers Hoag and Jensen; Blockman swore with gusto every time an opponent made a point. Lt. Will Sandin was an energetic little figure bobbing in and out of the surgeon's post hospital, where Sandin's wife lay in labor. Late in the day Trooper Hoag urged Trooper Van De Reuter to see the surgeon about his cough, but the little Dutchman ignored Hoag. Justin Harris spent the evening playing cards with the adjutant and three lieutenants. Harris had a run of luck and won thirty dollars.

Tuesday dawned brassy and turned hot by ten o'clock. The mail coach came and went, making a racket. Not long after the noon meal, a dispatch rider galloped into the quadrangle and Colonel Mallory walked outside to investigate the noise. Captain Mueller appeared in the doorway beside headquarters, a chunky figure, and came across to join the colonel. The dispatch rider stumbled coming up the steps and handed a crumpled sheet of paper to Mallory.

The colonel read it without hurry. The adjutant said, "From Ben Hannibal?"

"He has a party of Indians pinned down in a cul-de-sac. He's asking for reinforcements and supplies."

Mueller said, "Well, then."

"Captain, Lieutenant Sandin's troop should be ready for its patrol. Tell him his orders are changed. Write an order for the quartermaster and send Sandin's troop out with food and ammunition to reinforce Hannibal."

Mueller seemed about to speak, but held his tongue. Mallory was talking to the dispatch rider. "Take a fresh horse, Trooper, and guide Lieutenant Sandin back to Lieutenant Hannibal."

Mueller went toward the stables with the dispatch rider. Drew Mallory tugged his mouth corners down and went into his office. He found Pete Rubio slouched in a corner of the room. "How did you get in here?"

"Walked in," said the Chief of Scouts. "Got yourself a fishing pole yet?"

"Not yet."

Rubio followed him into the inner office. "Whereabouts Lieutenant Hannibal got this standoff?"

Mallory handed Hannibal's dispatch to him and went back to his desk. Rubio read it laboriously. "That's a box canyon sure enough. But I don't see no Apache riding in there without they had a good reason. Young Ben makes the mistake of following them in there too far, he liable to find hisself boxed from behind. Right between them that way he'd get cut up bad."

"I think he's smart enough not to go in after them. They can't get out as long as he blocks the entrance."

"Ever see an Apache move at night? They can get out. Well, I hope he gets him a piece of luck. He figures he got fifteen Apache pinned down in there, they probably fifteen, twenty more he never seen." Rubio went toward the door. "Got any chores for me right now?"

"No."

"Then maybe I hunt you up a fishing pole."

Rubio left. The afternoon crawled forward, and at six the sergeant major bulked over Mallory's desk, and Mallory was saying, "Haven't you found the adjutant yet?"

"No place around, sir. His horse is gone."

Mallory said, "See if Lieutenant Sandin's on post."

"Yes, sir."

Pete Rubio brought a pole in with a hook and coil of line. He left it standing in the corner and went away without a word. Twenty minutes later McCracken returned. "Lieutenant Sandin's in the post infirmary with his wife, sir. She's due any time now."

"Get your note pad, Sergeant."

McCracken went to the outer office and brought back a pad and poised a pencil in his great fist. Mallory dictated to him: "To Capt. John Mueller. The usual salutations. Body of the order to read as follows: You will turn over command of all troops in your jurisdiction to Lieutenant Hannibal. You will return immediately to Fort Dragoon where you will confine yourself to quarters until further action is taken. By order of. Take care of the formalities and prepare it for my signature. Get a dispatch rider saddled and ready to take it to him."

"Yes, sir. Colonel, permission to speak?"

"No."

McCracken's lips pinched. He saluted and waddled out.

Soldiers filed into the mess hall. There was a racket of dishes and pans. Mallory strode across the end of the compound, paused at his own house gate, and then walked on to the next. Beth Mueller's rose bushes grew thick along the white picketing; the lawn was heavy and dark, still moist underfoot from the daily ritual of watering. The sky westward was splashed with gold and blood; little balls of fragile white cloud scudded across the zenith. Mallory knocked and stood impassive until he heard footsteps coming forward within the house, and then he stiffened, for the sound was that of a man's boots. It was Justin Harris who opened the door.

Beth was at the end of the parlor by the fireplace, her head thrown back. Mallory took off his hat. His white hair seemd to darken the crags and hollows of his face.

He said, "I didn't intend to intrude. I suppose you already know what I came to tell you."

"Justin told me." Her face was drawn, strictly composed, revealing nothing beyond the strength of her will.

Harris said gently, "I'll be going." When Harris walked by, Mallory did not look at him. The door snapped shut.

Beth said, "I suppose you'll have no choice but to court-martial John." She turned her back to him and laid both hands against the mantelpiece, staring into the dark hearth below as if a fire burned there. "I wish he'd had the courtesy to stop by and tell me where he was going before he left. It would have made it easier for me to stand by him."

"Do you intend to stand by him?"

"I don't know, Drew." She dropped her arms, went to the divan, and moved her hand in a vague, absent circle. "Sit down —sit down. Don't stand with your hat in your hand like a moonstruck cowboy."

Mallory took a chair without smiling. Beth said, "If I thought he needed me, I might. Do you know we haven't had a conversation in months? All we talk of is trivial things. He's obsessed with the idea that he's got to see action. It's changed him. You can see that. He'd never have done it before. He's always been so reliable."

"Don't try making excuses for him."

"He's not a foolish man. Why has he done it?"

Mallory said bluntly, "Do you care that much?"

She turned her face toward him. "Maybe not." A nervous smile. "But I'd hate to think you forced him into it, Drew."

"I've gone out of the way to keep him on post. That's hardly what I'd call forcing him into action. He's not a little child to rebel against every order he's given."

"Are you sure you haven't put so much pressure on him that he had to break out?"

"I hardly think so. He's not a sensitive type."

"Isn't he?"

Mallory got up and walked to her. There was a small rush of evening wind around the house. "John's finished, Beth. You made a bad bargain. There's no use searching for causes or excuses. Either give him up or stick by him—you've got to choose."

Her answer was a while coming. "If I give him up, I don't want him to believe it's on account of this. He'd think I'd turned against him just when everything else went wrong—and because of it."

She reached for his hand and separated the fingers one by one; she pressed his palm to her cheek and said, "I don't know what to do. Help me."

"I can't say anything, Beth. Not until you've decided."

It made her push his hand away. "Sometimes your damned code of honor disgusts me. You and all the rest of them— doesn't anything matter but pride?"

"There's not too much else."

She shook her head. "I can't get close to you, Drew. I can't reach inside you any more." And when he said nothing, she murmured, "I think you'd better go."

He went back to the chair to pick up his hat.

"Drew? "

Her eyes were moist. She said, "Give me a sign. I need it—I'm not strong."

Mallory had a clipped, businesslike way of talking, but there were times when he pushed his words out with slow reluctance. "I wish I could."

On Thursday morning Drew Mallory sent a second dispatch rider after Mueller with a sealed order identical with the first. Anger was close to the surface of Mallory's eyes.

He was on the porch at midmorning when Justin Harris came along with his loping stride and his brash grin, undaunted by Mallory's smoking eyes. "It's a baby girl, and Sandin's bouncing around like a kid on a trapeze. Sent you this." He handed a cigar to Mallory, who pushed it absently into his pocket and frowned toward the desert. Harris drank from the *olla* cup and said, "Are we still leaving at noon?"

"What?"

"Those two Mexicans we were going to meet at the border."

Mallory said, "We'll have to wait. It may mean an all-night ride to keep our appointment."

Harris nodded and put a light to his own cigar. He said, "It was the act of a good man to take Sandin's place."

"It was the act of a disobedient fool," Mallory answered with no show of force. "Mueller had my orders and disregarded them. I don't see how you can twist that around to make him out anything but a poor soldier, Captain."

"Sometimes there's a difference between a good man and a good soldier, I guess."

McCracken came onto the porch and broke into the conversation. "Somebody coming out there."

Mallory looked past the main gate and saw a thin dust spire—a single advancing rider.

Harris said, "That will be a messenger from them. Do you intend to put him before a court, Colonel?"

"I do."

Harris regarded him stonily. The messenger advanced, slowly taking shape, emerging from his own dust cloud; his horse ran, so it appeared, on a thin shimmering curtain of light suspended just above the earth. They could see the rise and fall of hoofs, but the figure did not appear to be moving any closer. McCracken murmured, "Looks like trouble—he's killing that horse."

It was some time before the horseman swept into the compound, not pausing by the sentry. When he dismounted, his boot stuck in the stirrup and he cursed getting it out. The horse's eyes were round; its flanks heaved, and it was sodden with white lather. Its head hung down, its tongue out, legs splayed, trembling. Mallory said, "You've ruined that animal, Trooper."

The messenger was out of breath. He began to talk with an inarticulate rush of syllables. Justin Harris struck him on the arm. "Take it easy, Magruder." Harris dipped a cup of water from the *olla* and handed it to the man.

When the messenger drank, he spilled water down his chin; it ran down the front of his uniform, beading on the dust. He gave the dipper to Harris. "Lieutenant Hannibal's compliments, Colonel, sir, and he'd like for to have you send the surgeon out to Tilley's Ford. Captain Mueller took a bullet in the back last night."

Mallory said, "They're at Tilley's Ford now?"

"Not yet, sir. Coming back from the Piedras. They rigged a

litter between two horses for the captain, but Lieutenant Hannibal, he said he wanted the doctor soon as he could get him. They ain't moving fast, sir, on account of the captain and a couple other wounded."

"Anyone killed?"

"None of us. Killed some Indians. We lit into them right proper, sir."

Mallory made a quick gesture toward Justin Harris. "Captain, tell the surgeon to pack his kit. He'll need an escort—detail six men with a sergeant and tell them to saddle a horse for the surgeon. Tell the sergeant to keep a sharp eye—Captain Clayton's a first-class doctor, and I wouldn't want him jumped."

Harris began to move, then drew himself up and saluted elaborately. His eyes were hidden under the overhang of his brows. He went away on the run.

Clouds blew across the sky, and the sun moved over. At two Mallory was on the porch again with his revolver belted on. A sadded civilian horse stood tethered below. There was a broadcloth suit in the saddlebags. Justin Harris came out of the stables leading an ugly piebald horse rigged with a Texas working saddle. Harris's face was noncommittal when he climbed onto the porch, saluted, and stood waiting.

It was late in the afternoon before dust showed on the desert. Footsore, Harris was sitting irritably on the porch railing. He got up when the troopers rode in on sluggish, weary horses, the surgeon accompanying Mueller's litter. Two troopers wore wound dressings, bandages startling white against their uniforms. Ben Hannibal and the surgeon broke away from the column and dismounted. Hannibal's face was shrunken, the muscles tight and showing tautly through the skin like an old man's. He came forward on leaden feet while the surgeon stood in the dust with a bleak aspect.

Mallory exploded onto the porch, coming out fast and straight up as though on wheels. "How is he?"

"Bullet in the spine," said Clayton. "Cut the spinal cord, but didn't break any bones. I've got him splinted now, and I'll get him into a cast right away." The surgeon removed his hat, dried his forehead in the crook of his elbow, and gritted his teeth. "I doubt he'll use his legs again," he muttered, and walked away toward the post hospital where troopers were bringing down the litter.

Ben Hannibal had a strange flush on his wire-tense face, a strange shine on his eyes. He made his report in Mallory's office with the door closed. Harris sat in the outer office on the corner of Sergeant Major McCracken's desk; they had little difficulty in hearing through the door. Hannibal spoke in a deadened tone, and afterward Mallory said, "Let me get this clear. The Apaches were still in a corner when you withdrew, and you could have kept them there. Is that true?"

"It would have been costly, sir. They had better cover than we had, and once they began sniping, I knew we had only two choices. We could go after them, and that would've been hell—we'd have had to root them one by one out of the rocks, and the'd have cut us to ribbons. Or we could pull out. We couldn't stay put, because they had too good a command of our position."

"Then your position was badly selected in the first place. Did you pick it?"

There was a pause. Harris glanced at McCracken. Ben Hannibal's voice reached them faintly. "No, sir."

"Mueller picked it?"

"Yes. I was on higher ground when he came, but he decided to move the main party down closer to the center of the canyon mouth. He was afraid the Indians might slip past us in the dark unless we closed up the entire entrance. That's exactly what they tried, as it turned out, so I guess Captain Mueller was right—we were waiting for them when they came, and we held our fire until we couldn't miss. I counted eight Indian dead before they fell back."

"Then they went up the side slope of the canyon to higher ground instead of retreating into the canyon bottoms. Is that it?"

"Yes, sir. That's what gave them the advantage when daylight came."

"You should have been prepared for that."

"Yes, sir," Ben Hannibal said.

McCracken smiled slightly. "Good for him. The lieutenant ain't giving up nothing."

"Shut up," Justin Harris said.

Hannibal's voice was going on. "Captain Mueller was unconscious when I decided to withdraw, sir. I gave the order. I take the responsibility."

"It costs you very little to say that, Lieutenant. This is the second time you've turned away from a fight."

"It was that or lose a lot of men."

"But you had them boxed? They couldn't get past you?"

"No, sir. Not unless they killed a lot of us first. They had good sniping positions on the hillside above us. They kept us pinned down tight, wounded two of my men. And shot Captain Mueller. Tactically I guess you'd say it was a stalemate, but they had the advantage. They had a lot of rocks to shoot from. All we had was brush and one small hummock."

Mallory said, "Is it correct there was no water in that canyon?"

"Yes, sir."

"No water for miles in any direction. Is that right?"

"Yes."

"You'd killed their horses to prevent their rushing you."

"That was my scout's idea."

"All right. They had little if any water among them. I submit if you'd held out seventy-two hours they'd have surrendered to you for lack of water."

"Maybe they would have, Colonel, but they'd have killed quite a few cavalrymen in the meantime."

The sergeant major's fist was clenched tight on the desk top. He was leaning far forward, as if it aided his ears. Mallory said, "You're a soft man, Lieutenant. If you wish a transfer, I'll recommend you for it. If you want to resign your commission, I'll expedite it."

"No, sir."

"You don't belong here."

"I think I do, sir."

"As you wish, Lieutenant. I have no technical grounds for removing you from your assignment without your agreement. But I remind you, mister, that I can make it damned rough for you."

"Yes, sir."

"You intend to stay?"

"Yes, sir."

There was another moment of quiet. McCracken softly pounded the desktop. He spoke in a whisper between gritted teeth. "Good for him—*good for him*."

Mallory's voice was curled like a whip. "Then I'll have to toughen you up, Lieutenant. I'll assign every misfit and slacker and guardhouse drunk in this regiment to your troop. I'll saddle you with recalcitrants and cowards until you'll wish you were in the guardhouse yourself. I'll give you men who can't shoot, men who can't ride, men who spend every other day lining up for sick call. I'll give you the dirtiest-clothed and dirtiest-mouthed men I've got. I'm going to give you my halt and my lame, Lieutenant, and you're going to make Christians out of them— because mark me, I'm going to throw you to the lions."

McCracken was breathing in thin wheezes; his eyes had popped wide. Mallory's voice came level-flat through the door. "Do you understand me, mister?"

"Yes, sir."

"You'll take these men and you'll bully them into a fighting unit. You'll do it to save your own fair skin, mister, because I intend to put you in the front lines of every engagement we fight. You'll march twice as far and fight twice as hard as any other troop in the regiment. You'll have no more opportunities to back away. Now get out of here. You are dismissed."

Ben Hannibal came out, moving like a mechanism; if he recognized Harris, he did not show it. He went straight out to the compound and walked out of sight.

Mallory walked through toward the porch. "Is your detail ready, Captain? Let's go to Mexico."

# 7

· Between the Huachucas and the Patagonias a long yellow grass valley sliced down out of Arizona. At the end of it was Lochiel—a plaza with a covered well in the middle, cubic adobes around the square, old men squatting in doorways picking at their beards, and flatfooted women moving to and from the well with buckets, baskets, jars. Four armed Rurales stood at the inn with cartridge bandoliers across their chests, and six brown horses stood by.

Justin Harris rode beside Mallory, and behind them, bunched close, came the three-man detail: Cpl. Boone Blockman and two troopers. When they entered the plaza, one of the Rurales reached for the inn door and knocked. A fat man in khaki came to the doorway, picking his teeth.

Trooper Hoag held the horses. Mallory got down and Harris followed him, speaking to the fat man in the door. *"El General Kominski, por favor, Señor el Capitán."* Kominski was a colonel, not a general, but Harris had dealt with Rurales before and knew the protocol.

The fat man studied Harris and moved his attention to Mallory. "You will be the gringo *coronel*."

Harris rubbed a damp palm down the seam of his Levi's. Mallory, in a business suit, was headed through the door, but the fat Mexican captain stopped him. "And these?"

Mallory glanced at the four armed Rurales ranged along the wall. "And these?" he echoed.

The fat man laughed in his throat and stepped back. Harris followed Mallory inside. There was a crude table of long planks, overhung by a pair of ceiling-hung lamps. A man sat at the far end, gray of moustache and goatee, with the face of an eagle: shrewd clear eyes and a beak of a nose, a long, narrow, merciless face, angular and ascetic. "*Mi coronel*," said the fat captain in khaki.

Kominski wore a pale gray uniform and an infantry cap. He nodded. Mallory said to Harris, "Let's get started."

Harris said, "*El coronel quiere que—*"

"Speak English," said Colonel Kominski. There was a brief, brittle razor smile.

When Mallory sat, Harris took a seat and frowned abstractedly at the roughhewn planks, angry because, as it turned out, he was not needed here.

Mallory said, "I expected to meet Governor Pesquiera here."

"He was unable to come."

"Was he?"

"I am empowered to speak for him," said Kominski. His glance carried impatience.

"All right. I've come because we share a problem—Togomasai."

Kominski said, "You wish to urge me to attack the Apache strongholds in the Sierra. Wipe out the vermin's nest and the vermin will die. Is it not so, Colonel?"

"No."

Harris looked up and saw Kominski's quickened interest. Mallory said, "I didn't come here to beg favors."

Kominski arched an eyebrow and glanced at the fat captain. Harris turned his chair to have an unobstructed view of the fat man. Kominski said, "But then what is it you wish?"

It was stuffy and close. Mallory removed his hat and pushed his hair back with his hand. "I want you to allow me to enter Mexico with a cavalry regiment."

Harris sat bolt upright and stared at him. Kominski was frowning, and Mallory said, "I assume you've got reasons for leaving Togomasai alone. That's not our concern. The Apaches are a threat to us, and I want them stopped. I want free passage for my men in and out of Mexico. We'll ride to the Sierra, do our business there, and go home directly."

Kominski murmured after a while, "You make it seem easy."

Harris glimpsed the fat captain's guarded eyes and heard Kominski add, "It is not easy, Colonel. The people here remember the wars we fought against one another, not so long ago—many live who lost friends or limbs or fathers. They remember the emigrants of 1849 who raped, and the gringo scalp hunters who sold the scalps of peons for the bounty on Apache hair. They have no love for you, Colonel, the people of Sonora."

"I don't ask for it."

"Do you speak for your superiors, Colonel? For your government?"

"I speak for myself," Mallory said.

"Then we will have your word alone that you will bear responsibility for the acts of your men while they are in Mexico."

"My word," Mallory answered.

Kominski had a quiet, pebbly laugh. "Then perhaps it is possible that we may agree, Colonel. For I respect a man who breaks his own path."

Justin Harris held his tongue until they rode from Lochiel. Hens scattered before them and squawked from the roadside; dogs yapped at them. They crossed the border, and the fat captain in khaki sat there on his horse watching them ride north. Justin Harris said, "You could stand a court-martial for this, Colonel. General Sheridan won't back you up, and neither will the President."

"They will if we succeed, Captain."

"It's against the treaty."

"A few years ago Mackenzie raided into Mexico out of Texas. It was the same kind of thing. There was a little flurry afterward, but it died down. The Mexicans stand to gain as much as we do—they won't complain very loudly."

Hoofs rang on gravel; they crossed a stream. "How soon, Colonel?"

"Seventy-five days from now."

"What?"

"That's right, Captain," Mallory said. "A winter campaign."

"In those mountains? Sir—"

"Winter is the one time when we'll catch all the Apaches in camp. Otherwise half of them would be away raiding into Arizona while we leave it defenseless."

The sun was dehydrating, and their canteens were almost dry when they reached Quivari Tanque, planning to noon there and drink from the pool of captured rainwater. But Harris saw a dead cottontail rabbit by the near edge of the flat pool. "Wait a minute—hold the horses back."

He knelt to taste the water on his tongue; he spat it out. "Poisoned."

He mounted his horse and put a hooded stare on Mallory. Mallory said, "How far to the next water?"

"Seven hours northeast to Tinajas Prietas. Or six hours northwest to Puma Wells. Or six hours due east to Rice's homestead, but that was burned out and I don't know if his well's gone dry." Harris glanced at the sun. "The tank wasn't poisoned by accident, Colonel."

"I know."

"Probably Togomasai's men. A patrol. They must have recognized us. Too few to attack us, so they decided to poison us or just kill us by thirst."

"Then they've poisoned the other wells, too," Mallory said.

"Not all of them. They'd leave some of them alone so they'd have water for themselves."

Cpl. Boone Blockman spurred alongside. "Which ones, hey, Captain? God-damned puking Apache. I get my hands on one, two of them, you watch me wring their puking—"

"That's enough," Mallory said.

There was an abrupt rush of hoofbeats, and a rider broke out of a gully half a mile away, waving a rifle overhead. The horseman's shouts reached them on the wind. The Apache shook his rifle and wheeled away. "God *damn!*" shouted Corporal Blockman, and raised his boots to spur the horse into pursuit.

Mallory said, "*Halt.* Come back here, Corporal."

Blockman fought his horse down. "What the puking hell?"

Harris said, "They want us to wear out our horses chasing them. We'd make easier prey that way. Next time wait for orders, Corporal."

"Jesus, for all the—"

Mallory reined his horse around and all but rode Blockman down. "The next time you open your mouth, Corporal, it will put you in the guardhouse."

Troopers Hoag and Crane moved their horses forward, and
Hoag said, "What we going to do, Colonel?"

"The Indian rode northwest. We'll ride northeast."

With a dry, swollen tongue Harris folded his blankets at
sunrise and saddled his horse and wondered what it would be
like to die of thirst. They rode into the desert, and he rolled a
pebble around in his mouth, to activate the saliva. His lips stuck
together when he tried to open them. He thought, I might die
today. It surprised him that he felt no particular regrets. He
thought distantly of Georgia Bowen; for a while he had a very
sharp image of her face. It only made him think of Ben Hannibal, and that made him bitter.

At ten in the morning they came on two Indians. First they
found tracks, faint in the powdered ground. Little bunches of
dried yellow grass tufted the stone-cropped hills. There was a
spindle tracery of ocotillo, greasewood, and yucca, but no
water. The sun was the color of a polished bugle. Harris
dismounted to study the tracks, and his eyes lifted, following
them toward the horizon; the land buckled up in cross canyons
and steep hills. "Sandals—two men on foot. It could be a pair of
Apaches."

A growl throbbed in Boone Blockman's throat, but with his
eyes on the colonel, Blockman kept his peace. Young Trooper
Crane licked his lips and watched the rocks with fitful, darting
eyes. Trooper Hoag had his canteen halfway to his mouth
before he realized it was empty.

Mallory said, "How fresh?"

Harris was down on one knee. "Maybe half an hour, no
more." He felt his spirits lifting; he turned to his horse and
swung up with new energy. "If there's water around, they'll
know where to find it."

Trooper Hoag said, "They could be looking at us right now,
Captain."

They rode up a loose, steep hill and halted near the top.
Mallory held up his hand, got down, and crawled to the crest.
He lay flat, searching; he backed away and came down to the
others. Boone Blockman had lifted his rifle and balanced it
across his saddle horn.

Mallory said, "Two Apaches afoot. They're walking across

an open hollow down there. Let's take them alive." He mounted and spoke to Boone Blockman. "Put that weapon away and keep your hands off it."

They went over the top at a gallop. The Indians saw them coming, but there was no hiding place on the open flats. Both Apaches dropped to squatting positions, lifting their rifles. Mallory made an arm signal: the troopers spread into a loose fan, flanking him, and Harris galloped at his left shoulder. At the gallop, iron horseshoes rang on the rocky ground. An ocotillo's spines raked Harris's arm, tearing the sleeve.

He saw the smoke puffs and heard the reports of the Indian rifles. Trooper Crane cried out but kept his seat on the swaying saddle. Crane was pale, his face frozen into a mask of pain or fear, or both. He kept up only because his horse had the herd spirit of the run; the reins were loose in Crane's hand.

The Apaches had no time to reload their cap-and-ball rifles. Mallory halted within twenty yeards of them and trained his cocked revolver on them. One Indian dropped his rifle and swept up a knife. Fragments of bright reflection glittered along the blade. The second Apache grunted half a dozen syllables. Both then stood up; the first man dropped his knife reluctantly, and they clasped their hands above their heads.

Mallory said, "Tie them up."

Harris nodded to Corporal Blockman, who got down and walked cautiously forward with Trooper Hoag. Mallory glanced at Trooper Crane. Crane trembled; his face was white. Mallory said, "Tighten up, Trooper. All you've got is a crease in your fat."

A thin stream of blood darkened a bullet-burn along Crane's side. The trooper seemed paralyzed. Justin Harris reined close by and tugged Crane's shirttail out, pressed a folded handkerchief to the wound, and said to him, "You're not hurt. Hold this tight until it stops bleeding. Take it easy."

Crane's terrified eyes whipped around to him; Crane hardly seemed to recognize him. Harris took Crane's hand and placed it against the wadded handkerchief. "Hold that there."

Mallory was dismounting. Blockman had the Indians tied, back to back, with the four wrists bound together. Blockman's eyes were hot and round. He stepped back when Mallory approached.

Mallory spoke to the Indians. "Do you speak English?"

There was no reaction, and Mallory said, *"Hablan
español?"*

Harris came along and said, 'I expect they're lying."

"Maybe not. You don't speak Apache, do you?"

"No, sir."

Mallory said, "If we can't talk to them, they're no use to us.
Shoot them."

"What?"

"Shoot them."

"Colonel, for God's sake!"

Mallory said, "You can get that rifle of yours now,
Corporal."

"Yes, sir," said Blockman. He walked to his horse, satisfied.
Harris stood glaring at Mallory and knotting his fists. Blockman
came back, cocking his Springfield, and said, "Which one first,
Colonel?"

"Suit yourself."

One of the Indians was staring not at Blockman but at Drew
Mallory; the Indian's eyelids flickered, and, abruptly, Mallory
turned on him. "You've understood every word I said. If you
want to live, speak up."

"I hear," the Apache said grudgingly.

Mallory said, "Put the rifle down, Corporal."

"But—"

Mallory swiveled his eyes toward Blockman without
speaking. Blockman lowered the rifle hammer and hung the
weapon in the bend of his elbow. The Apache said, "I am fool.
You would no kill us."

"He thinks you was bluffing, Colonel," Blockman said.

"I don't need an interpreter, Corporal. Keep your bloody
mouth shut until I ask for your comments. You're on report as
of now." Mallory's hand lifted to the Indian's hair. He jerked
the man's head back and said distinctly into the Apache's
uplifted face, "I was not bluffing. You've poisoned the wells
against us. Some wells you did not poison. Tell us where there's
fresh water."

"No."

Mallory released the man. "Separate these two, Corporal."
While he watched Blockman undo the knots, Mallory lifted his

revolver and inspected its cylinder. The Indian walked two paces away from his silent companion and rubbed his wrists. Mallory said, "I will not waste time with you, Apache. Tell me where the water is. If you don't, I'll shoot your brother. If you don't speak then, I'll shoot you, too."

"You no shoot."

"Where is the water?"

"No water," said the Indian. *"No hay agua."*

Mallory lifted his revolver and sighted along the barrel, aiming at the second Indian's chest. The hills were silent, and the first Indian stood regarding him solemnly. "Speak," Mallory said. The Indian said nothing. Mallory pulled the trigger.

The solitary gunshot was deep and round, deafening. It pushed the second Indian back a loose step and dropped him to the earth, dead where he fell.

Shock held Justin Harris dead still. Mallory cocked his revolver and turned it on the surviving Apache. "You are no good to me if you do not speak," Mallory said. "Speak now or I'll shoot."

The Apache studied his dead comrade. Echoes of the shot swam in Justin Harris's head. Part of his mind wondered how he could record his feelings of the moment. The Indian on the ground was very dead. Not much blood issued from the .45-caliber wound in his heart.

The Apache said, "May the God of the Sun burn you to coal."

"And the water?"

"The water is fresh at the springs of the white man who keeps goats."

Mallory said to Harris, "Who does he mean by that?"

"Yaeger's ranch. About eight miles west of here."

"Do you think he's telling the truth?"

"I don't know," Harris said.

"We'll take him with us. If he's lying, we'll shoot him there."

Harris reached for his reins and said with quiet bleakness, "Pawns, Colonel?"

"Yes."

Boone Blockman herded the Indian forward. Blockman was shaking his head and repeating in a monotone, "Jesus God. Jesus God."

Ben Hannibal stood dismally in the long early shadow of the barracks and said, "I'll have to thank Captain Harris for lending you to me."

"You got a tough job, Lieutenant," said Sergeant Bodeen. "I like to help you out if I can."

"Fall them out and let's have a look at them."

Bodeen was an immense man. Stooping, he filled the barracks doorway. "Fall out. *On the double.*"

They came out past Bodeen, a ragged crowd—the derelicts and the unwanted of Fort Dragoon. When they took formation before the barracks, they made the most unsoldierly troop in Ben Hannibal's memory. They were tired because they had spent the night preparing for inspection. They were resentful because they had been assigned to the ugly duckling troop. They were disrespectful because their troop commander was Lieutenant Hannibal, young and green and, some said, a coward. They were angry because they all felt the army had treated them unjustly.

Ben Hannibal spoke to them. "You were told to fall out this morning in fatigue clothing for work details. I see four men in parade uniform. Don't you gentlemen have ears?"

Sergeant Bodeen back-paced a step and spoke out of the side of his mouth. "Mind if I talk to them, sir?"

"Go ahead, Bodeen."

Bodeen had a voice as big as his frame. "You four in parade uniforms. Fall out over here."

The four men looked around and moved forward slowly. When they were assembled, the sergeant said, "I guess you didn't want to work today, is that it? All right. We'll oblige you. You four go on back to bed."

Ben Hannibal watched and said nothing. The four men stood openmouthed, Corporal Blockman's voice growled from the formation: "Looks like we should've worn puking parade uniforms."

Sergeant Bodeen wheeled. "Step out, Blockman."

Blockman took a pace forward from the line. His gaze was defiant. The sergeant said, "If this is the kind of men they are, we don't want them working with us, do we, men? You—Corporal Blockman—you can go back to bed with these four."

"But I didn't—"

"Get back in your sack, Corporal. That's an order."

Blockman marched angrily up to the four men and led them into the barracks. A slow, crooked smile crossed Sergeant Bodeen's face, and the men of the troop began to laugh. Presently the laughter became hooting, and when Blockman's angry face appeared at the barracks window, the troopers waved sweetly and called out: "Nighty-night."

Sergeant Bodeen said, "Ten-*shun*." He about-faced and said mildly to Ben Hannibal, "It's one way to handle them, Lieutenant. If a man has any pride at all, you can shame him. Blockman won't live it down for quite a while. Watch now—the men'll be calling him 'Nighty-night' from here on in. And it's luck for us we caught Blockman out right off. He's tougher than the rest, and he has two stripes, and I hope the lieutenant ain't forgetting that an army corporal's the toughest man in the chain. A corporal's the meanest man in the army, and maybe he ought to be. He has more men under his direct command than any other rank, and he's the man says live or die to a trooper's face."

Ben Hannibal said softly, "Thank you, Bodeen. Let's march them around and trim them up."

Low clouds drove forward from the southwest, and Sergeant Bodeen dismissed the troop into barracks. Corporal Blockman stumbled to his bunk and tugged off his boots. He massaged his soles and complained, "Jesus. Two God-damned hours. Jesus."

Van De Reuter was combing burrs out of the little dog's fur. Bodeen stood in the doorway, perhaps the biggest man alive, and let his look of scorn travel the length of the room before he tramped away across the quadrangle. Corporal Blockman lay back on his mattress. "Puking ass army. Ain't got enough trouble, they stick us with the green one-bar and Bodeen for a chaser. Hell, giving orders on the right foot—wonder Hannibal didn't march the whole puking troop into the wall."

"Hannibal ain't so bad," said Trooper Hoag. "Ain't none of his fault. It was the old man put him up to it."

"Sure. I'll tell you something, boys, and it's a fact. Puking old man likes blood. He likes to bring a man grief. Out of Fort Griffin it was Mallory himself took a troop of Dragoons out after Comanche. Tracked them across the Llano Estacado, ran himself out of food, ran himself out of water, killed pret' near half the puking horses. Walked all night long and come up on the Comanches before daylight. Now nobody's had no sleep in two days and nights, so what's the old man pull? Sweet Jesus, the bastard orders a puking attack! Boys can't even see straight. Attack, he says. Attack."

Trooper Crane, who had a display of bandage along his bullet-creased side, sat across the room watching. Crane, like most of the rest of them, was new to the troop. He was very young, and he had a way of showing up for sick call whenever assigned to patrol detail. He said, "What happened then, Corporal?"

"What the puke you think happen, kid? They attack. Sure. They wipe out a couple dozen Comanches. But some good men died that day, kid, and one of them be my brother Leroy. Sure as you sit there, Old Man Mallory killed my brother like he shoved a Springfield carbine up his backside, sure as that. Mallory killed my brother. I can't put it no plainer. Brother and the rest of those boys so beat up and tired out they couldn't see, they couldn't walk. They was groggy as a week-long drunk, and the God-damned old man knew puking ass well they wasn't in no fit shape for fighting, but he done it anyways—he said attack and got them killed."

Blockman went on cursing. In the far corner Trooper Hans Van De Reuter coughed and wiped his lips. Trooper Hoag looked at him. Trooper Crane was rubbing the down on his cheeks, watching Boone Blockman with great shocked eyes. Blockman said, "The old man knows I know. He knows I know what he done to my brother, and he hates my puking guts. You can believe that. Christ, we's doing all right until Mallory showed up. Old King Cole was about to pin another stripe on me—you know that? Instead, I got turned down twice in a row for promotion by the old bastard Rock. You know what he says to me? You want to know what he says?"

No one encouraged him. Blockman climbed to his feet and threw his shoulders back, tucked his chin in, and tried to imitate Mallory's voice.

"Corporal Blockman, you got a reputation around this-here establishment for drinking, hot temper, and general unreliability. I'd be doing this here exalted regiment no favor at all by grantin' your *re*quest for a promotion to sergeant. Go out and kill me twenty-five Injuns, and then maybe I'll give it some *con*sideration." Blockman guffawed without mirth and sat down. "First time I try to take a shot at a God-damned Apache the old man practically skins me alive. He says, 'No shooting,' he says. He says, 'We'll take them alive.' he says. So we don't shoot, we take them alive, and the old man hisself gets the pleasure of shooting his Apache cold. Jesus Christ—at least the puking Injun had a *gun* when I went after him."

Someone laughed halfheartedly, and Blockman wheeled. "You think it's funny? I tell you one thing—I don't think it's so puking funny my brother got killed. One dark night old puking Mallory not going to make it home. And I ain't just whistlin' about that, Hoagy—you can mark—"

"That's enough." It was a gruff voice, and it belonged to Bodeen, who had come to the doorway. "Get your boots on and fall out."

"Oh, Jesus H. *Christ,*" said Blockman. "What the puke *now?*"

Justin Harris left the stable, said something to Pete Rubio that made the Chief of Scouts laugh, and parted ways with Rubio. Ben Hannibal stood by the barracks, watching his troop fall out; Harris went that way. He stopped in the shadows while Ben Hannibal walked forward and Sergeant Bodeen said smartly, "Tensh-*hut!*"

The troop straightened, a ragged line, and Bodeen dressed it up. Ben Hannibal walked along the front rank, performing a cursory silent inspection. He reached the end of the line and swung away, walking out in front of the troop, turning unhurriedly to face them. Harris watched the chunky lieutenant fill his chest with air and push his shoulders back.

"There's not a polished button on one of you. Gentlemen, a cavalry trooper wears twenty brass buttons or more. The next time you fall out I expect to be blinded by them. Commencing after tonight's mess, we will have two inspections a day. Any man who doesn't pass can expect extra work. Dismounted drill this afternoon was disgraceful. You are all confined to the post with no town privileges, until further notice. The sutler's bar is out of bounds to every man of you. No man is to leave the post without written permission from me. I've instructed the adjutant, and the sentries will not allow any of you to pass. In one week I'll review the situation, and it may be that you'll win the right to leave the post at that time. But one man out of step can keep the lot of you out of the saloons on Saturday night. Remember that."

The troopers stared, disbelieving. Thirty feet away by the Rec House door, Justin Harris watched, his hatbrim pulled down over his eyes.

Ben Hannibal said, "When I dismiss you, you will march to the stables and see to your horses. You will soap your saddles and clean your gear. After mess there will be a mounted inspection, and God help you if I find a spot of rust on any man's bridle bit. Inspection will be followed by one hour's close-order mounted drill on the flats below the east gate."

Ben Hannibal about-faced abruptly, turned the troop over to Bodeen, and watched the sergeant march the troop to the stables. Hannibal's shoulders sagged. He came over to the Rec House with a sour expression and glanced bleakly at Justin Harris.

Harris said, "You're overdoing it a little."

"The guardhouse brigade. I've got damned little time to make anything out of them. The old man's got me slated for patrol in eight days. Two of them have deserted already. The old man was right about one thing—if I want to keep my skin, I've got to train them to the point where I can depend on them. I can't go after Apaches with half my men drunk and the other half ready to turn tail. I gave them three hours on the firing range today and it was disgusting—most of them couldn't hit the broad side of a barn from inside the barn, Justin. They need every minute's practice they can get. I've got them digging their own slugs out of the target backstops and scrounging gunpowder from God knows where—they'll be up half the night tonight reloading cartridges."

"You can't do it too fast," Harris warned. "The colonel's pushed them pretty far already. He's been smart enough to know just how far he can go before they collapse. You be careful, Ben."

"Aagh," Ben Hannibal said, dismissing it. "I want to stay alive, damn it. Come on—I'll buy you a beer."

They took a table in a quiet corner of Maldonado's cantina. Ben Hannibal had a second beer and a third; he watched the clock hands crawl around. A splash of sunlight hit the floor through the open entrance and lengthened into the room. Talking desultorily, Ben Hannibal's tongue grew thick. Suddenly he slammed his empty mug down on the table with a display of force. "Damn it, quit looking at me like that."

"Like what?"

"I wish to hell you wouldn't act so God-damned friendly. I cut in on you—why don't you ever say something about it? And for God's sake don't tell me you like to mind your own business. Every time you look at me you're thinking about Georgia. You make me feel like I'm twisting a knife in your back."

"Forget it."

"How?"

Harris leaned toward him. "What's really bothering you, Ben?"

Hannibal shook his head, and Justin Harris said, "Was it that patrol with Mueller?"

"Damn you," Ben Hannibal growled.

"Your first blood," Harris said. He sat back, watching. "Something happened. It wasn't what you'd expected it would be. At first you got a little scared. Then you began to feel you had to prove how brave you were, and that made you more scared."

"You make it sound so God-damned simple."

"I didn't mean to."

Ben Hannibal said, "I killed four Indians that day. Four. I shot three of them and ran a sword through one. He was lying on the ground with a bullet in him, and I didn't have to do that."

Harris studied him. Ben Hannibal's eyes had gone fever-bright. Harris said, "You tasted it, and you liked it."

Ben Hannibal whispered, "Yes." He dropped his chin on his hands and brooded. "Damn it, yes—yes."

"You can't make any judgments from your first time under fire."

Ben Hannibal talked as though he hadn't heard. "I didn't hate them. How can you hate a man you've never seen before? You talk about 'the enemy,' and it's just something out of a manual on tactics, something abstract, like your opponent's chessmen."

"Everybody enjoys winning, Ben."

Ben Hannibal cried: "It isn't just a silly God-damned game!"

"Maybe it is—maybe it is."

Ben Hannibal covered his eyes and sat motionless. In time he said, "I heard about Mallory shooting down that Indian. You were there. Didn't it make you feel anything, Justin? Anything at all?"

"Maybe regret."

"Didn't you get mad?"

"For a little while."

Ben Hannibal lowered his hands and stared at Harris bitterly. His mouth worked a few times, and finally he said, "I'm going to marry Georgia as soon as I can, Justin, and I've just discovered one thing. I don't feel sorry for you any more. You can go to hell on skids for all I care." He got up and walked out.

Harris took his time finishing his beer. It had gone warm and flat. He went out blinking into the brightness of the afternoon and thought, rather dryly, there are more things kicking around hereabouts than are dreamed of in my philosophy. His long legs took him around through the garrison gate to the infirmary. He found Captain Clayton in the office and said, "Any change in Captain Mueller's chances?"

"No," said the surgeon. "And there won't be. You people are doing no good by pestering me."

"Pretty certain he won't walk again?"

"I am."

Harris said slowly, "I think, if it had been me, I'd rather the bullet had killed me."

"I doubt that." The doctor added angrily, "Why are all of you such confounded heroes? My God, I should think you'd be glad to be alive no matter what the circumstances."

"If life were all that mattered, we'd all be grubbing around like apes."

Clayton said, "That's a strange thing for you to say."

"Is it?" Harris went outside into the broil of sun, thinking about John Mueller, who was now, in the phrase currently going around the regiment, just half a man. Gallantry and honor and nobility and pride—was everything artificial, beyond survival? It was odd to think about these things.

Going toward the headquarters office, he passed Beth Mueller crossing the compound. He lifted his hat and regarded her with an expression that halted her, turned her around, and made her stare at him. Abruptly she laughed. "Justin, you look like a tongue-tied ingenue."

"I thought of a half dozen things to say, none of them any good."

"The world hasn't ended. You men are so jealous of your physical abilities. It's as if a man without legs were dead."

"Isn't he?"

"He is not. You're in the grip of codes and values that are none of your own making. All of you. I think you're all infants and fools."

He stood with arms akimbo; his bony elbows made scarecrow joints of his sleeves, and he watched Beth Mueller go up to the surgeon's and disappear inside. Ben Hannibal left the stable, dusting off his sleeves; the huge Sergeant Bodeen followed him, and the two talked briefly, Ben Hannibal's arm riding up and down as he spoke. Bodeen went back into the stable, and Ben Hannibal crossed the quadrangle, stopping long enough to say to Harris, "You'd think none of them had ever seen saddle soap before," and going on, dragging his shadow behind him. Harris felt angry with Ben Hannibal for having stirred up questions inside his carefully insulated mind.

His face took on a waspish look. A group of children played hide-and-seek outside the gate; they scattered when "I" Troop rode in from the desert. From the bored look in Lt. Will Sandin's dust-reddened eyes, Harris knew the patrol had turned up nothing of interest. Sandin went into the office to report. Shortly he came outside with his lips pursed into a rosebud. Spying Harris, the garrulous bantam lieutenant came over and said, "We are in the hands of a God-damned despot." His eyes mirrored a vast resentment. When Harris made no response to his opening gambit, Sandin grumbled another phrase and went off to his quarters. Sergeant Major McCracken came out, hurrying on an errand, but stopped long enough to salute carefully and speak irreverently. "Ain't you got nothing better to do than stand in the sun, Captain?"

McCracken waddled away. Harris had the feeling that everything was rushing past him today. He couldn't get a grip on anything. Ordinarily things passed him by without leaving a mark: he did not allow himself to be drawn into things, and he took pride in the thought that he had not lost his way back out of the maze. But the walls frightened him now; they crumbled.

He formed a loose fist and went toward his quarters.

## 8

Fragments of talk cruised through the night. A sentry walked solemnly back and forth before the guardhouse, rifle tipped across his shoulder. On Mallory's porch Justin Harris studied the chessboard and observed, "You're sacrificing pawns again. I suppose I'd better look out."

"Always do that, Captain," Mallory said drowsily. When he was tired, he had a way of pushing back his white hair with both palms, stretching the skin tight around his eyes. He moved a chesspiece. "Go ahead."

Harris considered his moves. He batted a moth away and put only half his mind on what he said. "Don't you ever loosen up, Colonel?"

"What?"

"Does anybody ever call you by your first name?"

Mallory didn't answer. Harris made a move. "How's that?"

"A little better." Mallory leaned forward, casting a shadow across the board. "You're learning. You think you have a hard taskmaster, don't you? You're remembering that Indian I shot down in cold blood. You think I was dead wrong to do it."

"It made the other Apache take us to fresh water."

"Of course. But you can't help suspecting there might have been another way."

"I haven't thought much about it."

"I've had the same suspicion," Mallory said. It made Harris

glance sharply at him. The colonel said, "The man in charge learns one thing, Captain. At times he has to make snap decisions and stick by them for the rest of his life. Sometimes it's more important to be able to make the decision than it is to know whether it's right or wrong."

"Maybe."

Mallory touched a pawn but did not move it. He droned sleepily through the night; the air was soporific, and momentarily his guard was down. "An officer in war learns one thing immediately: A man can take infinitely more than you give him credit for."

"Is that why you shot the Indian?"

"Possibly."

A trooper walked by, and when he was gone, Mallory said, "I had a small party of recruits tagging along with some dragoons going to reinforce Grant at Vicksburg. We were crossing a hill —I think it was somewhere between Jackson and Columbus. Bedford Forrest's irregulars routed the dragoons we were following. They retreated, if that's the word. Without horses we couldn't keep up. I recall it was freezing cold—a week before Christmas, the eighteenth of December. I had a sorry green collection, not much more than a platoon, with a ragtag assortment of muskets and horse pistols. The lieutenant and I had the only two revolvers in the party. Most of our ammunition blew up when the Confederates exploded our wagons. They had a little brass three-pounder. I dug us in on a hilltop, trenched full-circle. Bedford Forrest was no man for a standing fight—he had bigger bones to dig up. He left thirty cavalry to clean us off the hill. If they'd been smart, they'd have smashed us up with the three-pounder, but Forrest's men were guerrillas and they didn't have much conception of artillery. We drove off a couple of direct assaults. After dark they got the idea to use the brass gun on us. I think they fired about a dozen explosive shells and hit us with five or six. Blew up half my men in their trenches. I had no medical supplies, and we had to watch four or five men die of wounds that shouldn't have killed them—we had no water to drink, let alone clean wounds. The enemy peppered us half the night with grapeshot. After midnight we tried to break out on foot, but they had us ringed with sentries. One of them gave the alarm, and they drove us back to the trenches. By dawn I believe I had sixteen men left out of the forty I'd started with. The lieutenant wanted to surrender."

Mallory paused, moved a pawn, and folded his hands around his knee. Justin Harris said, "Why didn't you?"

"Bedford Forrest wasn't inclined to take prisoners."

"Did you try?"

"I didn't, no. The lieutenant thought he might. He walked down in the morning under a white flag. Someone shot him down. I doubt it was done under orders, but it gave the rest of my men the resolve to fight it out. We had to hope another column of reinforcements would happen by. Of course, no such thing happened, but the hope was pretty strong."

"How the hell did you get out of it alive?" Harris asked, and thought of a similar story Pete Rubio had told him recently. Rubio claimed he had been surrounded by a party of Indians and had run out of ammunition. Harris had asked, "What happened?" and Rubio had answered, dead pan, "They killed me, of course." It had amused Rubio to get the better of him. But Mallory wasn't that kind.

Mallory moved a pawn; Harris pushed a rook forward. Mallory said, "We were pinned four days on the hill. No one had any sleep. I couldn't breathe for the sulphur smoke. It rained on the fifth night, hard enough to cover us—we simply walked through their lines. I regretted we had to leave four badly wounded men to be captured. I've no doubt they were killed on the spot the next day. We'd had no food in three days and no water in four, except what we could drain out of canned fruit. We hiked a full day. One of my men sighted smoke, and we came on a field where there'd been a skirmish—dead horses lying around. We made a meal of that. All in all, it was a stalemate. We'd kept a sizable enemy force busy for the better part of a week, and that might have been important in the balance against Grant. We'd used our ammunition well—I judged we inflicted a dozen casualties or more on the enemy."

Mallory added offhandedly, "I had the satisfaction of blowing up their three-pounder while we were slipping through their lines." He made a move on the chessboard. "Of course, I was young. If I were in that situation today, I'd play it differently."

"How?"

"You can do any number of things. The idea is to convince the enemy you're doing one thing while actually you're doing something else. Make noise in one place while you crawl your main body out in another direction, belly-flat and without noise. Divert the enemy's attention—it's a classic rule, of course. I used it on you in a few chess games. If you read Caesar's War Commentaries, you'll find one of the few times anyone put something over on him was when the Massilians set fire to the Roman siege-works and managed to distract the Romans long enough to get to their own shelter."

Mallory added, "Of course you have to consider all the facets. A trick that would fool an army of hill farmers in Mississippi might not fool an Apache. You have to tailor your tactics to the nature of your enemy."

Harris said, "The idea behind most of these schemes is to sacrifice a few men to give the rest a chance."

"Often there's no better way." Mallory watched Harris push a knight across a dog-leg in the board pattern. Mallory said, "If I take that knight, I can't protect my queen. Is that what you have in mind?"

"I guess I'm not playing too well."

"You're improving. A month ago that move wouldn't have occurred to you."

Harris thought, a month ago I wouldn't have cared. He wondered why it was suddenly important to stand up to Mallory.

He said, "Tell me something. Am I the only one here who plays chess?"

"You're the only one who has a chance to learn by it."

Harris said slowly, "I don't think I know you at all."

"I'm afraid my life is all of a piece. I'm a soldier."

"You can't just step into a uniform and throw away all the rest."

"Perhaps I had nothing else to throw away."

Harris said, "I asked you before whether anybody ever calls you by your first name. Is that your answer?"

"I had several close friends during the war," Mallory said. "Most of them died. One of them took a bullet in the face and fell right across me."

"And you want no more friends. Is it that simple? That's too cut-and-dried for me."

"About all there is," Mallory said, "is the satisfaction of doing your job well. Here—you're in check."

Harris interposed a pawn between his king and the threatening bishop. Mallory said. "That's a sacrifice move. I thought you disapproved of them."

"Not in a chess game," Harris said.


The November sun was not particularly dazzling. The troop sat asaddle on the parade ground. On the porch Will Sandin watched them with a sardonic look. Ben Hannibal came out of the office, his face strained, thrusting his written orders inside his blouse. Sandin said mildly, "Good luck, Ben."

Hannibal nodded to him before going down, picking up the reins, and mounting his horse. Sergeant Major McCracken came outside by Sandin. They watched the troop drum away, and McCracken said, "First patrol for that crew."

"They're a dirty bunch. I wouldn't want to have my life in their hands."

"I'm thinking Lieutenant Hannibal can handle them," McCracken said.

The ugly duckling troop ran across the desert at a steady pace. It took them a day and a half to reach the bend of the Smoke. The men took their ease in a brief noon camp under the cottonwoods. The trees were turning; autumn came late on the desert. Bodeen, massive and monumental, checked horse gear methodically. Corporal Blockman had found something to complain about with deliberate profanity. Trooper Hoag frowned at the rippling river, and young Trooper Crane looked as though he regretted that his bandage, a badge of honor, had been removed.

· Ben Hannibal sat smoking under a tree. He could see his scout, John-Ben Mingus, out on a promontory. Mingus looked like a hunter's dog casting for smells. Ben Hannibal's thoughts were angry; he had found death in a new form this morning. Corporal Blockman's words still hung in his mind: "Sure enough, this God-damned country got to have its puking man for breakfast." Only this morning's breakfast had been not a man but a woman, an old dried-up Mexican woman with a leather-hilted Apache knife lodged between her back ribs so tightly that its owner had been forced to leave it there. Corporal Blockman had broken down and wept. "She couldn't even bleed with the puking knife in her, couldn't bleed it out. Must've tooken the old scarecrow a long, long puking time to die." Buzzards had taken the old woman's eyes.

It still had not settled well on Ben Hannibal's stomach. He remembered John-Ben Mingus talking to him. "You got to remember, Lieutenant, they's two sides. Mexes and whites been taking Apache prisoners for a hundred years. Making slaves out of the boy Indians and whores out of the girl Indians. Giving them diseases and what-all. Somebody kidnapped your daughter and sold her to a whore house, you'd get mad too."

Ben Hannibal watched the latticework branches make delicate shadows on the ground. He said, "Mount them up, Bodeen," and went to his horse. The ring of Bodeen's powerful voice echoed along the riverbank. Men splashed forward, and John-Ben Mingus trotted down the hill to meet them as they broke out of the trees and swung away from the river. Mingus was part Negro, part Arapaho, and, he claimed, part Russian; his father had been a fisherman out of Sitka, he said, but if so, he had only his mulatto mother's word for it. His skin was the hue of old clay tile. All his thin bones were intolerably long. Like a caricature of Don Quixote, he rode a small appaloosa horse with his bony bare feet almost touching the earth. He had hollow cheeks; he might have been forty-five or seventy. As a scout he had no peers except Pete Rubio.

Ben Hannibal rode away from the column to meet Mingus. "Any chance at all, John-Ben?"

"Not the way y'all going. They've done gained an hour since we started after them."

"Still headed east?"

"I reckon."

"They can't go too far that way."

"That's a fact, Captain," said Mingus. Mingus called all officers Captain—even youthful lieutenants, even Colonel Mallory.

Mingus added, "Three more hours running east, they hit right dab into the San Esteban reservation. They don't want no part of them Agency police."

"Then they'll have to turn off, somewhere between here and the Mogul. North or south."

"Or double back, Captain."

"No. They've seen our dust behind them."

"It's a big bunch, Captain—maybe thirty. They might figure to jump us."

"I doubt they'd try it in open country. The question is, will they swing north or south?"

Mingus reached out with his bare toes and uprooted a yellow grasslike stalk. He bent his leg, transferred the stalk to his skeletal hand, and put the stalk in the corner of his mouth. It waggled when he spoke. "Don't pay to try second-guessing an Apache."

"Guess anyway."

"Well, was I taking bets, I'd consider this bunch been raising hell nigh on two weeks. They prob'ly getting tired and hungry for home cooking. And I'd think about one other thing, too—them wagon tracks where the old woman got killed, and the burnt-up wagon in the gully there."

"What about them?"

John-Ben Mingus said, "You don't figure the old lady was driving that rig by herself, do you, Captain?"

Ben Hannibal wiped his dry mouth. "You think they may have taken a prisoner or two, then."

"Could be. And if they wasn't expecting to head right home, they wouldn't take no prisoners."

Ben Hannibal had a look at the troop. He caught Bodeen's questioning glance. Horses stood dashing their tails at river-bottom flies that had followed them. Ben Hannibal said, "You think it's a good bet they'll turn south?"

"I do," said John-Ben Mingus.

Ben Hannibal muttered like a man talking to himself. "It's a long border, but there aren't so many places where a group of men could get across without being seen. What do you think?"

"I think if we're still behind them they'll split up and fade across one by one. Otherwise, they feel safe enough, they just might cross over in a bunch. Most likely at night. And I know your next question, Captain, but I got no answer. Ain't no telling where you might set a trap for them. They just too many places to get across at night."

Ben Hannibal grunted absently. He was looking south across the desert. "A man on Morgan's Peak, John-Ben—how far could he see with field glasses?"

"Thirty mile, to the north."

"If they go south, they'll have to cross that desert strip. If you stood on high ground, you'd see them coming."

A slow grin spread across John-Ben Mingus's skull face. "You a sly dog, Captain."

Ben Hannibal made a signal to Bodeen. The big sergeant rode forward, and Ben Hannibal said, "I'll want a three-man detail. Assign Van De Reuter to it and anybody else who's sick or slow on a horse. I want them to rope-drag a lot of brush behind them. They're to ride northeast for five miles, then cut due east and ride to the reservation. That will take them the rest of the day. Keep them off the skyline, but I want a lot of dust—that's what the brush-drag is for. If there's any sign of trouble, they're to run for cover. At the reservation they can hook up with the main detail and accompany it back to the fort."

"Smart," commented John-Ben Mingus.

Bodeen left without a word. John-Ben said, "Them Apache see a line of dust north of them, it'll herd them south. Unless they decide to ambush your three-man army."

"There's risk in everything you do, John-Ben."

"You want to set a trap, you got to get there ahead of them. That mean you got to turn southeast now. They bound to see our dust going down that way."

"Not if we ride in the river," Ben Hannibal said.

Ben Hannibal was the son of a schoolmaster in Joplin, Missouri, and it amused him to speculate that it might be a necessity of fate that made a soldier of a Hannibal who came from a place only fifteen miles from the town of Carthage.

At five the troop left the river, half-drowned in its spray, and picked a careful path across rock flats, keeping to the hollows. The sun, going down, made a slow explosion of vivid colors. The troop waited impatiently in a meadow, and John-Ben Mingus took the lieutenant's field glasses and rode his game little horse up the steep side of Morgan's Peak. Sergeant Bodeen loomed. "I never heard of anybody taking an Apache by surprise, Lieutenant."

Ben Hannibal said evenly, "We'd better eat now, Bodeen. There may be no camp tonight. Cold rations and no smokes."

"Yes, sir," Bodeen said, and if he felt rebuffed, he gave no sign of it. Bodeen was an old campaigner, and Ben Hannibal knew what was running through Bodeen's mind: that the green lieutenant had been tested only once in battle. The sergeant's lack of confidence might be untactful, but it was excusable. Ben Hannibal was in high spirits.

Twilight grew deep. It began to seem as though John-Ben Mingus had been gone a long time. Cpl. Boone Blockman was chewing a matchstick. He suddenly slapped Trooper Hoag on the shoulder. "Hell, what I wouldn't give to be in Miz Madden's place about now. Hoagy, you know that little black-haired cooze from Louisiana? Sweet, sweet God."

Trooper Crane, with unshaved fuzz on his round cheeks, listened closely to the talk of these men. Trooper Hoag said, "Right now I'd settle for a beer and a smoke. Women's grief—grief and trouble."

"That ain't the way I hear you talk the other night at Miz Madden's, you puking liar." Boone Blockman slapped his knee and laughed.

Bodeen said, "Quiet down, Nighty-night." Someone tittered.

The moon drove away dusk. John-Ben Mingus rode into camp. "They coming sure enough, Captain. Look like they headed for Weaver's Canyon."

"How long do we have?"

"Two hours, maybe. We make it easy if we don't give ourselves away. Happen they get sign of us, they'll scatter like quail."

"I want to box them up," Ben Hannibal said with sudden fierce strength. "This time we'll have the high ground. Take us around the back way, John-Ben."

There was a thick richness of yellow grass, silver in the moon wash, rippling in glossy waves when the wind touched it. John-Ben Mingus said, "Weaver's Canyon just over the top now, Captain."

Ben Hannibal halted the troop. "Have a look, John-Ben."

The little appaloosa pony, a long way from its home in the Northwest, humped furiously upslope, urged by the flapping legs of its rider. In the waiting troop, horses fidgeted, and Bodeen said, "Steady now." Ben Hannibal caught the massive sergeant eying him speculatively. Hannibal thought angrily, what do they expect? What do they want? John-Ben Mingus came down and said, "Plenty of time yet, Captain. They still out on the flats, headed for the canyon. Reckon your brush-draggers fooled them good. They riding all bunched up like they alone on the whole desert."

Ben Hannibal tugged his lower lip. "Bodeen."

"Sir?"

"Horse holders to keep the animals here. Keep eighteen men with you on this side. Give me fifteen minutes to cross to the far rim with the others. Then spread your men at twenty-yard intervals along the top. Belly-down and in the shadows where you can. Hold your fire until I start to shoot. Understand?"

Bodeen nodded. "Lieutenant?"

"What?"

"You going to warn them?"

"No."

Bodeen's head pushed back. Ben Hannibal said, "Detail your men."

"Sir," Bodeen responded, and went back through the troop, calling names: "Devlin, Cord, Turvey—"

Ben Hannibal said, "Take us across, John-Ben."

He dropped off six troopers to hold the narrow head of the canyon. Crossing the narrow throat of ground, he watched the downhill gorge carefully. A pulse throbbed in his neck. Along the far side he deployed his men on the rim and settled in the boulders. They had an unrestricted field of fire along two hundred yards of sloping canyon floor. Then a cloud crossed the moon, and he could not make out the bottom. He felt sudden anxiety; he cursed softly. He thought he heard a pebble clatter in the canyon. John-Ben Mingus flopped down beside him with a long, angular buffalo rifle. Ben Hannibal looked upward at the heavy cloud and felt enraged. Mingus murmured, "Heads up—heads up."

The cloud passed by the moon. In the sudden pale light he saw a slow line of shadows riding up the steep pitch of the canyon. He tensed, blinked, bit his cheek. From nearby came the clicking of a Springfield's sidehammer drawing back to full cock. Ben Hannibal started, Mingus's eyes shone alertly, but the wind did not carry the sound into the bottoms. The silent group of riders continued its unhurried ascent. "Not yet," Ben Hannibal said. "Not yet."

John-Ben Mingus said, "They got a prisoner, Captain. Fourth man from the front. Look like a Mex."

"How can you tell?"

"Way he sit his horse. Must be the wagon driver."

Ben Hannibal's hatbrim turned. John-Ben Mingus said, "No way to get word across the canyon to Sergeant Bodeen. You going to let them pass?"

Ben Hannibal chewed his tongue. "No," he said. "No."

His hands were locked tight—he could not work the mechanism of his carbine. Sweat burst out on his forehead. The line of shadow horsemen advanced toward a point directly beneath him. He heard himself say, "Not now. Let them come on."

Mingus said, "You oughtn't to wait too long."

"A little farther, John-Ben."

"Might be hard to explain if that prisoner gets killed. Maybe you ought to let them through."

Ben Hannibal had trouble getting the word out between his teeth: "No." His hand clenched in a spasm. The carbine went off, slamming his unready shoulder in recoil. Dazed, he rocked back. He heard the deafening boom of .45-70's volleying to either side. Across the canyon Bodeen's rifles opened up. Muzzle flames lanced down into the gorge.

Down on the bottoms the grouped horsemen broke in wheeling confusion. Two riders pitched from their mounts. One of them, he was half certain, was the Mexican prisoner. Ben Hannibal pulled trigger and realized he had not reloaded the breech; the hammer clicked dully, and he flinched against an expected blast that did not come. John-Ben was talking calmly, but he couldn't make out the scout's words. The wind cut across his face, carrying the acrid sting of powder smoke.

He lowered the carbine's trapdoor breechblock over a cartridge and sought a target. Shadows scurried into the rocks and an answering fire commenced, small-bore and large-caliber weapons mingled, orange tongues of quick flame licking upward from the canyon deeps.

Bodeen's men laid down a murderous fire. Ben Hannibal heard someone's lusty, obscene shouts—perhaps Cpl. Boone Blockman; his ears singled that voice out of the racket.

He saw a running shadow and fired and knew he had pulled too hastily. The feeling of urgency tightened around his groin. John-Ben Mingus was shouting, and he said, "What?" and heard John-Ben say, "Move, damn it—move!" before John-Ben's buffalo gun roared with a wrathful boom. A bullet from below, half spent, chipped a white triangle from the rock by Ben Hannibal's hand and screamed off. Comprehending, he rolled away to a new position, bruising his knee painfully. Powder smoke choked his lungs. He blinked and coughed.

Mingus said, "They'll spot your powder flash. Keep moving around. Better make some noise over that way, Captain." His arm stretched out, pointing. "Indians there. Climbing up toward Sergeant Bodeen."

"I don't see anything over there."

"You bound to trust my old eyes, Captain. You got thirty Apache bottled up down there, and they see the sergeant only got sixteen, eighteen rifles. They forming up right now to rush him."

"I thought they had no stomach for night fighting."

"They ain't got much choice right now. You want to try to blast them off that hill?"

"It's a big hill. If you can't see them, how do you hit them?"

Mingus did not answer. Ben Hannibal said, "We'll have to go down there."

"You crazy?"

"I'm going down there."

"You got nerve where your brains ought to be, Captain."

Ben Hannibal fired and reloaded. He stood up. *"Form on me!"*

Someone shouted. A hard shoulder rammed him down. John-Ben Mingus untangled himself. "All right, you a brave bastard. Jesus."

Ben Hannibal sucked air into his chest. He saw the crouching troopers gathering around. He said, "Bodeen doesn't know it, but they're climbing up after him. We're going down. Load and follow me. Keep spread out."

"Sweet Jesus!" said Trooper Hoag.

"Be careful who you shoot at," Ben Hannibal said. He started down.

Ten paces down the pitched slope, he realized he was alone on the hillside. He wheeled. A bullet churned by, and he said in a reasoning way, "Well, come on."

No one moved. An anonymous voice said, "You be a hero, Lieutenant. We're just the guardhouse brigade. We'll sit and watch."

Ben Hannibal said savagely, "Shoot that man!"

A barrage of rifle fire started up from the lower edge of the far slope. Ben Hannibal dropped to his knee and answered it. Corporal Blockman's voice hurtled toward him: "God-damned puking ass fool! Come back here, Lieutenant."

A red blaze colored Ben Hannibal's vision. He fired at the powder flames below, dropped his carbine, and stood up. He shouted irritably: "Come on—Come on." He ran awkwardly downhill, tugging at his revolver. Blood pounded in his head, and he heard himself shouting. Down on the Indian position lifted an intensified roll of gunfire. Someone whooped. Ben Hannibal dropped to a crouch, sighting along his revolver barrel. In back of him someone uttered a ringing cry, a rebel yell.

He heard the massed pound of boots stumbling down the slope. Blockman was still cursing him—"You stupid God-damned puking fool!"—but Blockman's voice was getting closer. He swung and yelled at them, "Spread out, you idiots. Follow me down."

They dived to either side of him; he was caught up in their howling rush. Across the canyon Bodeen's men caught the unreasoning fury of it; they stumbled down the bank, firing deliberately into the shadow Indians trapped on the bare open slope.

Indians ran, Indians lay flat, Indians rode horseback. From the head of the gorge the six troopers of the detail fired straight down the trough into the whirl.

Ben Hannibal windmilled his arms, running down, trying to stop his momentum. An Indian on horseback galloped up across the slope at an angle. Unable to avoid the collision, Ben Hannibal leaped upon the Indian and crushed the man's head with his revolver. He fell off the staggering horse in a tangle with the Indian, kicked himself loose, and struck a rock with a bone-crushing crash. The Indian rolled loosely downhill. Ben Hannibal pounced upon him and found that the man was dead. In a rage he slammed his revolver down once more against the Indian's head.

Ahead of him troopers swarmed onto the uneven canyon floor, engaging the Apaches, fighting lustily. The night was a smashing of bullets, a crying of voices. A riderless horse galloped near; it reared and screamed with a half-human voice. Ben Hannibal was close enough to see its eyes roll. He knelt to fumble shells into the revolver's clumsy loading gate.

Trooper Crane loped downhill, off balance. Crane sailed by like a rock out of a sling and tripped, sprawling. When the young trooper started to rise, he cried out and fell back. Ben Hannibal crouched by him. "What is it, Crane?"

The trooper's answer was carried away on a crash of concerted fire. The night filled with color—the red-orange-yellow darts of sulphuric gun flame, like a display of Roman candles. Half blinded, Ben Hannibal steadied his revolver upon a running breechclouted Indian twenty feet away. He fired across the prone youth. The Apache went down with a bloody hatchet in an outstretched fist. Ben Hannibal said, "What?"

"I think my ankle's bust, sir." Trooper Crane went into a fit of swallowing.

Ben Hannibal reached for Crane's feet. "Which one?"

"Left one, Lieutenant. Jesus, you better leave me—you got a fight. Oh, God!" Crane's head rocked back.

."It's only a sprain, I guess. But you can't walk on it."

"No, sir. I'll wait here."

"You can't. Come on." He took the youth's arm over his shoulder and got him upright. An Indian ran by; Ben Hannibal fired and missed. He moved ahead, half-carrying Crane, wielding the revolver in his free hand. He saw the night in a series of bright static cameos, still images lighted by muzzle flashes like lightning bolts. A struggling rush swarmed everywhere. A burly private sat in a cross-legged position, coolly and methodically working the lever of a captured repeater rifle, with the corpse of an Apache at his feet. A trooper with a bloody head crawled forward on hands and knees, evidently blinded; as Ben Hannibal watched, the trooper fell on his face.

In the half shadows not far away an Indian was loading his
cap-and-ball musket with a ramrod. The Indian looked up,
reversed the rifle in his grip, and fired while the ramrod was still
in the barrel. The rifle blew up in the Indian's face, but the
ramrod went arrow-like through Corporal Blockman's arm and
lodged there. Blockman became speechless with anger. Ben
Hannibal lost sight of him in the swirl.

Trooper Crane said, "Sir?"

"What?"

"Your head's bleeding."

Ben Hannibal felt of his head. His fingers came away from
his ear wet and warm. He said, "To hell with that." With
numbed awareness he saw John-Ben Mingus jump like a dead
frog and fall with a dark hole above his right eye. Ben Hannibal
did not have to go closer to know the old scout was dead.

A bullet glanced off his belt, tearing a slice out of the leather,
bruising his flank. He roared an incoherent sound.

Bodeen's men seemed to have boxed a party of Indians
against a narrow cliff. Most of the racket now came from that
quarter. Bleeding warmly from his earlobe, Ben Hannibal
lurched in that direction, carrying the hobbling young trooper.
Crane hung on his shoulder and shook with weeping. His cries
made great choking, sputtering sounds. An Indian was crawling
up the slope and Ben Hannibal shot him in the back. Singly and
by twos, a number of Apaches rode away at a dead run—up the
sides, down the canyon northward—all pursued by bullets. One
of them left the saddle as though plucked upward by a fist. Here
and there a shadow climbed the barren slopes. Ben Hannibal
emptied his revolver and stopped to reload it. He stumbled
forward again and came upon a wounded Indian lifting a knife.
The blade glittered, outsize in the moonlight. The knife came toward Ben Hannibal's leg, and Ben Hannibal swung his revolver,
raking the sharp front-sight across the man's eyes, laying his
face open. The Indian's knife whistled back and forth in great
blind arcs. Ben Hannibal kicked the Indian in the face and
hacked brutally at the man's skull until the Indian collapsed.

Ben Hannibal stood over him spread-legged, head hanging
down, lungs burning. Crane's arm clutched him around the
neck. There was a single ragged aftervolley. He heard a distant
fading drum of hoofs.

# 9

Trooper Crane tugged his sleeve. "Is it over now, Lieutenant?"

Ben Hannibal turned a full circle, frowning in a puzzled way. His eyes grew wide; suddenly he was afraid. "I guess it's over, Crane. I'll give you a boost up—come on."

It had not occurred to him that he ought to rally the troop around him. Instead, he went to find the troop. Men were gathered below the narrow cliff, around the towering shadow of Bodeen. Ben Hannibal carried Crane that far and set the trooper down. Bodeen said, "You want me to call the men in, sir?"

"Call them in and get the horses down here." His voice croaked. He wiped a hand across his eyes, thinking of the Book—Cooke's *Manual of Cavalry Tactics*. "I'll want a head count as soon as possible, Bodeen. Post sentries and gather the wounded."

"Yes, sir." Ben Hannibal couldn't tell whether it was contempt or only weariness in Bodeen's voice.

Ben Hannibal braced his shoulder against the cliff. He was afraid because he did not know whether anyone besides John-Ben Mingus had seen the Mexican prisoner before the shooting started. John-Ben was dead. There was no one else, he thought, who could testify that he had known the prisoner was in the line of fire. He calmed himself.

Cpl. Boone Blockman wandered into sight drunkenly. He had somewhere discarded the ramrod that had pinioned him. The pierced arm was wrapped in the torn-off sleeve of his blouse. Bodeen's voice bellowed in the dark, a beacon for the scattered

soldiers to home on. Corporal Blockman walked up to Ben
Hannibal and spent a while trying to recognize him. Someone
was crying. Blockman said without preamble, "You God-
damned crazy puking ass, starting down that hill all by
yourself! Didn't you see they wasn't nobody going to follow
you?"

"No," Ben Hannibal said, "I didn't see that."

"Sweet Jesus."

"You followed me, didn't you?"

"Hell, I guess you'd have gotten killed if we hadn't."

"Well," said Ben Hannibal, "thanks, Corporal."

"Sure."

Men crowded up. Blockman muttered and wandered away
from him. "Puking God-damned heroes." Ben Hannibal pushed
away from the wall and for a moment thought his legs were not
going to support him. The troop sergeant loomed. "Ten
Broeck's dead, Lieutenant, and Capewell's dead."

"And John-Ben Mingus is dead," Ben Hannibal said softly.

"Yeah. Him, too."

"And?"

"Pillow's going to be dead inside a half hour. Slug in his lung.
Turvey I give a fifty-fifty chance—he's hit in the chest, but it's
pretty high. I ain't made a proper count of the wounded yet, but
they's one or two won't be able to travel too good. Don't seem
to be nobody missing."

"Does that surprise you, Sergeant?"

"Yes, sir. I'd have bet an arm some of these buckos would've
gone right over the hill."

"So would I," Ben Hannibal muttered. "What about the
Indians?"

"I ain't sure we got them all counted yet, Lieutenant. I make
at least fourteen dead. They lugged some wounded away."

A wave of dizziness surfed in Ben Hannibal. "We'll make
camp up there, on top. Double sentries. I don't want our horses
stolen. In the morning we'll take care of the Indian burying." It
was not his own voice talking, not his own will forming the
words. He felt absented from himself. His tongue said, "Wrap
our dead in blankets. We'll carry them back to Fort Dragoon.
Rig litters for those who can't ride."

He turned like a sleepwalker and lurched toward the high

ground. Someone caught him and put reins in his hand. "Here's your horse, sir."

He climbed into the saddle. His fingers were still locked around his revolver. The wooden grip was sticky: he had to disengage his fist with the fingers of his left hand. Clouds scudded by, freeing the moon, and when he looked back he saw exhausted men straggling behind him. Farther down there were shapes huddled in the deep bottoms of the canyon.

He stood on the hilltop with an arm hooked over the saddle for support. His men made camp. There was little talking. Bodeen came by. "Funny thing, Lieutenant—just found a dead Mexican down there, must've been with the Apaches. Maybe a renegade, maybe a prisoner."

Ben Hannibal said nothing. His throat pulsed. Bodeen said, "You got blood all over the side of your head, sir."

"It's all right. See to the others." He felt like a fool. "Bury that Mexican and put a cross over him."

Someone struck a match, and Bodeen snapped at him irritably, "Put that out, you damned fool."

The insistent scratch of digging grated unreasonably on Ben Hannibal's nerves. He covered his ears and felt the cake of blood on his wound. He felt a pulsing sting in the flesh of his ear. It seemed to have stopped bleeding. He watched the activity around him with the stubborn concentration of a drunk peering into a kaleidoscope.

Bodeen returned. "Seventeen dead 'Paches all told, sir, and we got two prisoners, both wounded. What you want to do with them?"

Kill them, he thought without heat. But what he said was, "Treat their wounds if you can. Tie them up. We'll take them home with us."

"Yes, sir. Trooper Crow's got four bullets in his right leg. I don't rightly know how he managed that. His knee's smashed and his thighbone, too."

"Can you splint it?"

"I got two men doing that, but I don't guess anybody's going to save that leg. I seen them like that before."

The remark seemed a rebuke. But Ben Hannibal was past caring; he only said, "Well, do the best you can for him."

"You ought to let go that horse and lay down, Lieutenant."

"All right."

He did not sleep. He lay suspended as though drugged until he was roused by a loud, fast flurry of gunshots and angry shouting. He blinked against vivid stabs of nearby muzzle flame. He rolled over and fumbled for his revolver, not finding it immediately; he clawed for it in a rising panic. It did not immediately occur to him that in the peppering of explosions he could not distinguish foe from friend. He shot bolt upright and brandished his revolver impotently, cursing, mouthing a rapid babble of incoherent obscenities. A bulky figure rushed past him in the darkness. He could see the shadow bodies of men rolling out of their blankets, seeking weapons. Loud, anxious questions howled, unanswered.

The gunfire quit as abruptly as it had begun. Hoofs rushed away; somewhere in the distance lifted a high, disembodied laugh. Ben Hannibal ran forward along the canyon rim, crashed into Sergeant Bodeen, unsettled the man, and reeled back. "What the hell happened?"

"God-damned Indians tried for the horses," Bodeen said in disgust. "Callaghan fell asleep, and they got past him."

"Did they get the horses?"

"No. We drove them off."

Ben Hannibal exploded, "Callaghan! *Callaghan!*"

"All right, Lieutenant," Bodeen said. "Callaghan's paid for it. He's dead."

"Sweet Jesus," Ben Hannibal said, picking up a phrase he had heard somewhere that night. His shoulders sagged. "Count heads, Sergeant."

Bodeen muttered a seasoned oath and filled his chest. "Troop—fall *in*."

Ben Hannibal sought Callaghan's rumpled corpse. He found it and stood glaring at it until Bodeen had called the roll. Bodeen came looking for him and reported, "I guess nobody got hurt but Callaghan. I'll go out and see did we do any damage to the 'Paches."

"What time is it?"

"About two."

"Saddle and get ready to ride."

"Ride? Where to?"

Ben Hannibal bellowed, "After *them!*"

"You can't do that. You got wounded to carry. How in hell you going to follow them in the dark without a scout?"

Ben Hannibal wheezed. He said resentfully, "All right, all right."

Corporal Blockman came out of the night, his arm sling-hung and a carbine across the bend of his elbow. He looked at Callaghan's body. "Couple dead Indians out there," he said, and went on.

Someone began to yell not far away, and Bodeen swung around. Ben Hannibal said nervously, "What the hell is that racket?" The man continued to yell, and Ben Hannibal broke into a run. Bodeen followed him, making a lot of noise with his boots. Ben Hannibal reached the head of the narrow cliff where the Apaches had made their brief stand earlier; he emerged between a pair of boulders and found a trooper on his knees at the edge. Bodeen demanded, "What you caterwauling about, Hoag?"

"Turvey fell off here just now."

"Turvey? What the devil was he doing over here?"

"Little off his head, I guess. I seen him get up and start flapping his arms when the shooting commenced."

"He's got a bullet in him." Bodeen swore and crouched to peer out over the edge. Ben Hannibal came up and looked. Bodeen said, "I think I see him. Right there, fifteen, twenty feet down. See?"

Trooper Hoag said, "Must be caught on an outcrop. You think he's dead, Bodeen?"

"How in hell can I tell?" Bodeen lifted his head and shouted, "Somebody bring a torch over here."

It was a while before anybody came. Bodeen said, "Turvey, you hear me?"

Ben Hannibal said, "He must be out."

"Out or dead."

A trooper brought a stick with rags wrapped around one end. Bodeen said, "Who's got a match?"

Ben Hannibal stirred and found matches in his pocket. He struck one on a rock and held it to the ball of rags. The torch caught fire and burned an evil red. Something fanned the air by his cheek; there was a crack and whine behind him. In the corner of his vision Ben Hannibal caught the flash of a rifle across the canyon. Bodeen said, "Jesus!" and flung the torch over the cliff and dropped flat on his belly. Ben Hannibal stood indignantly angry, rooted to the spot. Hoag, behind a boulder, said, "You better get down, Lieutenant.

The rifle didn't fire again. Ben Hannibal said, "Bodeen, send a couple of men over there to silence that damned Indian."

"Lieutenant, that whole hill may be crawling with them."

Trooper Hoag said, "You'd think they'd know when they was licked. We killed nineteen, twenty of them tonight. How many's left, for Christ's sake?"

Ben Hannibal said, "There's probably just one of them over there."

"Don't count on it," Bodeen said, and added, "sir."

Ben Hannibal dug grit out of the inside corners of his eyes. He pinched the bridge of his nose, and after a while he said, "Bodeen, bring me a rope."

"What?"

Trooper Hoag said, "You out of your mind, Lieutenant?" He was still behind the boulder.

Ben Hannibal said, "Now, Sergeant. Now."

"That's a limestone cliff, sir. You go down there and you be a sitting duck. They'll see you bright as day against that rock."

"Turvey's got to be brought up."

"Jesus, Lieutenant, ain't nobody going to —"

"Go," Ben Hannibal roared.

Bodeen went away in a hurry. Trooper Hoag said, "Turvey's all shot up, Lieutenant. Maybe he's dead. What you want to chance your hide for?"

Ben Hannibal had to think about it. He said under his breath, "You never buy somebody without paying the price for it."

"What?"

"You are one of my men, Hoag," Ben Hannibal said. "And so is he."

Bodeen came back and dropped something at Ben Hannibal's feet. "Rope," the sergeant said curtly.

"Tie one end to something."

"Nothing here to tie to."

"Then wrap it around your waist, Sergeant, and brace yourself."

"Lieutenant, by God, I don't—"

*"Bodeen!"*

Bodeen said in a lower tone, "Yes, sir." He tied a small loop in the rope, hooked it around his wrist, and fisted two turns of the rope. Ben Hannibal dropped the coil over the edge and stuck his head out. "Turvey—tie the rope around yourself and we'll haul you up."

There was no answer. "Turvey—damn it, listen to me."

Trooper Hoag said, "He ain't going to answer, Lieutenant. He's dead."

"I wish to God *I* was certain of that," Ben Hannibal said, and reeled up twenty feet of rope. He doubled it and tied it to his belt.

"Don't take too long about it, Lieutenant," Bodeen said mildly. "I ain't no Samson."

"You may have to be. Don't slip, Bodeen."

"You better hope to God I don't."

Ben Hannibal turned around to look at him. He saw that a silent knot of troopers had gathered. Bodeen made another attempt. "You could call for volunteers, Lieutenant."

"Do you think I'd get any?"

"You just might be surprised, there."

Trooper Hoag said weakly, "I'll go down after him, sir."

"You're shaking like a leaf, Hoag. You'd slip and break your neck. That's a sixty-foot drop."

"Yes, sir," Hoag said, and then said stolidly, "Better me than you, sir."

"No. Anybody else?"

No one spoke. Ben Hannibal walked out to the rim again and stood there as if awaiting a bullet. Trooper Hoag and one or two others walked over to Bodeen and gave Bodeen a hand holding the rope. Bodeen said, "You gentlemen ain't got nothing better to do, line up along the rim and shoot back at any guns you see open up on that far side over there."

Ben Hannibal tested the rope. He got a good grip on it and even at this distance saw sweat standing out on Trooper Hoag's face. Corporal Blockman settled down on the rim with his carbine, aiming it one-handed. "Puking son-of-a-bitch," Blockman said, to nobody in particular.

Ben Hannibal went over the edge slowly, feeling his way. The moon struck the pale cliff a glancing blow; he could see his shadow. He felt the rope slide a little and burn his palms. There was a flicker of light down below where the torch, which Bodeen had tossed to the bottom, was still burning. The flame made the drop appear miles deep. He thought, I could let go now and drop right into hell. His grip locked, and for a moment he was unable to move. He heard Boone Blockman talking. "Puking God-damned ass heroes," and he thought, I tend to agree with you, brother.

His feet found purchase in a crag, and he lowered himself, balanced there, easing his weight on the rope. Someone peered at him over the edge of the cliff. He turned his head to look across the canyon and disloged his hat against the cliff; it sailed away, planing on the air currents like a vulture in flight. He went on down the rope until his feet punched Turvey's flesh. Sergeant Bodeen said, "Tighten up, damn it. What in hell you boys think I am—a tree?"

Ben Hannibal lowered himself alongside the stricken trooper.' "Turvey?" Turvey didn't answer. "Turvey, God damn you, are you dead?" Turvey lay back in a broken arc across a jutting knob of rock. Ben Hannibal pried his feet under Turvey's ribs to have a place to stand. He called, "Relax a minute. I'm standing fast."

The rope slacked. Ben Hannibal crouched and touched Turvey's face. "Christ, Turvey—are you *dead?*" No, he thought, the bastard's breathing, the son-of-a-bitch is breathing, God damn him. Turvey's hoarse labored puffs seemed hearty enough.

"He alive, Lieutenant?"

"Yes, he's alive."

"Well, for God's sake!"

"Shut up," Ben Hannibal said. He was trying to puzzle out a way to get a grip on the man and yet keep both his hands free to hold the rope. Finally he pried Turvey up to a sitting position, got his shoulder into Turvey's belly and heaved. He had one arm around Turvey and the rope in both hands, but then he loosened up. I'm not that God-damned strong, he thought angrily. What the hell do you think I am?

Boone Blockman said, "Tie the puking rope around your boot, Lieutenant, and stand in it."

"Well, all right," he said. He made a loop in the rope and

stepped into the stirrup. Turvey almost slipped off his shoulder. He said, "Haul away."

The rope tautened, and he cried out immediately. His knuckles were scraping against the cliff. "Wait a minute—wait a minute." I'm not going to lose my fingers for you, Turvey, not for the likes of you, he thought. He had one foot free, and he pushed himself out away from the cliff. "All right, pull." The rope lifted him a few inches, and he rolled sideways against the cliff, one shoulder abrading the coarse rock. "To hell with that," he muttered, and kept kicking at the cliff to keep his body from scraping it. Turvey's weight on his back was more than it should have been. The rope tightened around his foot like a vise. He felt dampness against his cheek; Turvey's chest wound was bleeding on him. Turvey coughed and muttered something that Ben Hannibal didn't catch.

The rifle across the canyon began to fire. It triggered a deafening volley from the rifles over his head. His head was bent down under Turvey's weight, and all he could see was the torch burning down at the bottom of the cliff. The rope heaved, and he swung like a pendulum. He began to believe the rope would saw off and break. He listened to the clanging of bullets against the limestone, and something he had heard as a cadet came into his head: "The ones you can hear don't hurt you." He waited for a bullet to knock him off the cliff; he pictured himself dead. hanging by his right foot. He thought, now I know the taste of killing and the taste of dying.

A hand gripped his wrist, and at that precise instant a bullet jarred him somewhere and he cried out. They lifted Turvey from him, and he clawed his way over the edge. "I'm hit," he said.

"No, sir. The bullet hit him."

"Him? Who?"

"Turvey. He's dead now, sir."

Bodeen came up, and Ben Hannibal saw the great raw welts on Bodeen's wrist. Bodeen said, "Right through the back of the head."

Ben Hannibal rolled around and shook Turvey's shoulder. "Turvey, God damn you, you can't be dead."

Bodeen said, "I know how you feel, sir."

"The hell you do."

On the far rim the Indian rifle quit firing. Ben Hannibal said,
"Let's get out of here." He didn't wait for anyone. He went
along, his boot heels skidding on the pitch of the slope.
He passed the carcass of a horse and caught the smell of it.
Large wings flapped when he came by, but the bird didn't leave
its clinging perch on the horse's neck. Ben Hannibal watched it
hook its beak toward the horse's eye. He shot the bird with
his revolver and went away from there, listening to the chugging
of his own breathing. The half-light made a cathedral of the
gloomy canyon, turrets of the boulders.

The day was cool and brassy. The troop traveled at a slow
gait, accommodating its wounded. At eight Ben Hannibal
remembered to send a dispatch rider to Fort Dragoon with a
written report:

Engaged enemy Weaver's Canyon, killed at least 19,
suffered casualties of five dead and three wounded, one
seriously. Estimate arrival Ft. Dragoon noon tomorrow.
Request doctor for wounded trooper meet us at night camp
Crabb's Junction. '

Most of the day Ben Hannibal rode with his head tipped
forward over his chest. He felt like a man sentenced to execu-
tion. They nooned on the Smoke. The water ran ankle-deep
through a bed of sand between clay cutbanks. The desert
stretched away in all directions, and Ben Hannibal had the
feeling, looking at the uptilt of the plains, that he stood at the
center of a slippery anthole, sliding down. He ate in savage
stillness. A roadrunner zipped through camp, making a racket
like a pigeon, and presently Ben Hannibal realized that Bodeen
was talking to him.

"I reckon they did pretty good for a pack of no-goods. We
put together a fair troop out of them."

"It's your troop, Bodeen. I'm just along to carry the bars."

"Not after last night," Bodeen said.

"Sure," Ben Hannibal said softly.

The surgeon met them on the Smoke River, and Ben Hannibal watched him untie the wrappings and splints that bound
Trooper Crow's leg. The doctor worked by firelight, his face

giving away nothing. When he came away, Ben Hannibal stopped him, and the surgeon said, "I'm going to saw off his leg. He's not going to like the idea."

"No alternative?"

"No."

"I'm sorry," Ben Hannibal said in a dull voice. He went over to the wounded trooper and talked to him. The stilted conversation did not lift his damp depression. But after a while Trooper Crow said, "It ain't easy for you, Lieutenant. I don't mind."

"I wish I could do something, Crow."

"Never mind. I ain't worth crying over. Ain't nobody going to care about Gus Crow's leg one way or the other. Don't be taking the blame, now, Lieutenant—you did good. It's the first good lick we ever got. You fight like hell, Lieutenant. I never see nobody fight like you. I seen you run down that slope when they was all shooting on you."

Ben Hannibal said, "Well—" and stopped. Then he said, "Crow, in God's name why do you care about my conscience at a time like this?"

Trooper Hoag came up with a skinful of river water, boiled over the fire. The surgeon was unpacking his kit on a tarp. Trooper Crow watched all this and said, "Get away and let me alone with these buzzards, Lieutenant. I don't want you to watch this." His hurt eyes stared at Ben Hannibal with such force that Ben Hannibal recoiled. He went to stand a little distance away, and he thought, I never spoke five words to that man before this. I never knew his first name. The surgeon's saw grated against the bone of Crow's leg.

Trooper Crow's cries pierced the night. Ben Hannibal's tongue shaped the names of the men who had died: Ten Broeck, Pillow, Capewell, Turvey, John-Ben Mingus. He stood on the edge of camp with the high campfire laying down his shadow very long and thin. He felt he was in a cage; he threw himself against its bars. He heard a final sigh from Crow, who then fell silent. In time the surgeon's voice droned. "Take that away and bury it," and the surgeon came over by Ben Hannibal stretching. "He'll live."

"How high did you have to cut?"

"Above the knee."

"The poor bastard."

"That depends on your point of view. Mueller might envy him—Mueller's got two legs, but he can't use either of them."

"I can't feel sorry for him," Ben Hannibal said.

"Only for yourself," the surgeon murmured. "Don't fight so hard, Ben. Let things happen."

"Keep your mouth off me," Ben Hannibal said viciously, and rammed away into the dark.


Ben Hannibal made his report, and Colonel Mallory asked only one question at the end of it. "When you opened fire, did you know they had the Mexican with them?"

There was a brief moment when Ben Hannibal wished to stand as an oasis of honor. In the end he said, "Yes. I did."

Mallory said, "I'll want to see you later. Write up your report."

Ben Hannibal said slowly, "Is that all, sir?"

"That's all."

He went outside, feeling dull; he walked to the sutler's and drank several beers. An aging captain, McQuestion of "A" Troop, came in and talked for a while. Ben Hannibal did not hear much of what he said. McQuestion ran out of things to say and stood by the door, looking worried. When the captain left, Ben Hannibal had the feeling McQuestion was going after someone—Justin Harris, or perhaps Georgia. He made a face but did not leave; he kept drinking.

People went in and out of the bar. Some troopers entered to buy tobacco. Their eyes went wide, and they went out whispering and casting backward glances at him. And so, he thought, now I'm a God-damned legend on top of everything else.

Justin Harris came into the sutler's reluctantly and walked right up to him. Harris's eyes were half closed in wedges; he did not look happy. He said, "McQuestion said you were here."

"I don't need a puking wet nurse."

Harris put on an exasperated expression. "What's wrong now?"

"Nothing."

"I heard about the fight."

Ben Hannibal said, "It will go down in the records as a minor skirmish, and in three months it will be forgotten."

"Well, just what in hell do you want?" Harris demanded.

Ben Hannibal gave him a bleak glance and said, "Not a damned thing."

"You go after everything like a man trying to kill flies with a shovel."

"Oh, Christ, not you, too. I had enough of that from the surgeon."

"Quit playing a tough act."

"Tough?" Ben Hannibal looked surprised. "Jesus, I'm not tough. I feel like a God-damned vampire, that's all. I give myself nightmares."

"Just quit thinking about it."

"Sure—sure." Ben Hannibal thumped his empty beer mug impatiently on the bar and waited for the sutler to fill it.

Lt. Will Sandin came; it was obvious he had not just happened by. Uninvited, he joined them at the bar and rushed right into a speech. "I heard all about it, Ben. You've had all the damned luck. We've had only two engagements all year, and you've been in the thick of both of them. I heard how you crawled down that cliff to save a man. That's the kind of thing they stamp out medals for. You've done your career a lot of good. I believe congratulations are due."

Sandin held out his hand. Ben Hannibal gripped it absently and turned back to his beer. Not put off, Sandin went right on, turning momentarily sour. "I wish I had some of your luck." Then he brightened. "Don't mistake me—God knows I don't begrudge you any break you can get. You'll be going a long way."

Sandin clapped Ben Hannibal on the shoulder and turned his face away, ostensibly to call the sutler for a round of drinks; but his averted face was bright with envy.

Ben Hannibal wheeled from the bar and walked out. He heard Sandin's startled talk. It faded away behind him. He went along Suds Row and made a circle around the edge of town to Georgia's cabin. She wasn't home; he took down a whiskey bottle and lay on the bed.

She awakened him with a hand on his shoulder. He felt jittery; he shot bolt upright. Georgia picked up the bottle from the floor. It was dark outside; she had lit the lamp. She put her palm to his forehead and told him, "Go back to sleep."

"I guess not." He swung his legs over and sat on the edge of the bed. She was close by; he reached for her hips and swayed her toward him, turning the side of his face against her stomach. Her fingers laced his hair at the back of his head. Through the thin dress he felt the warmth of her belly. He said, "I'm going through hell. I don't want to drag you with me."

"Never mind."

She turned. He watched her slender movements. She sat aside on the end of the bed, drew her knees up, and left the skirt where it fell back. She said, "Maybe we ought to start all over, Ben. You decide what you want, first."

His hands dangled, wrists over his knees. He was not ready to answer. He believed she was crediting him with too much. He said, "I wish I was so much more for you—better, cleaner."

"I should be the one to say that. But I don't want to. Ben, it wouldn't work. We live in different worlds."

He stood up. "I guess we do. I guess so." He began to leave. With forced levity Georgia said, "If you're ever in my world, drop by sometime." He watched her blankly. Her eyes were wide and dry. Ben Hannibal dropped his head and hurried away.

# 10

She said to Justin Harris, "I used to have a rule—do what you want, and do it with whoever you want to do it with, but make sure it doesn't start to mean anything. I broke that rule with you, and I guess it became a habit."

"Do you want him back?"

"No." She was smoking, squinting through the haze at the guitar player. There were a few customers in the cantina. Harris was the only one at Georgia's table, and she was not dealing the cards. She said, "He didn't love me. He needed me. He doesn't need me any more, that's all."

"I wonder what he does need."

"And I wonder what difference it can make to you."

"It matters," he said.

"You've come all the way around to where you started."

"I just got sidetracked for a while, that's all."

She said, "Let's go somewhere."

"All right." He took her arm, and that surprised him; after a moment it pleased him. He guided her outside. Lamplight was mellow on the town; when they paused in front of the hotel, she had an agreeable smile and a rich warm tone of flesh. Justin Harris said, "There's only one thing I know for certain. Everybody's scared."

She looked lidded and drowsy. "I'm not. Not right now." She turned her face up. "The nights keep getting longer."

"I know."

"Take me home, Justin."

He turned and walked her past the side of the hotel. He said, "You know, I think that—"

"Don't talk," she said. She stopped and rested her palms against his chest. "Don't talk. Just love me."

Sergeant Major McCracken found Ben Hannibal at the stables. McCracken rubbed his enormous paunch. "Begging your pardon, sir. Colonel Mallory's compliments. He'd like you to come around the office if you got the time."

"It must be bad news to make you so polite, McCracken."

McCracken's face was impervious. "I ain't privy to the colonel's intentions, Lieutenant."

"No. I guess nobody is." Ben Hannibal put away his currycomb with unduly slow care; he brushed off his hands and went out. It was just sunset.

The clouded scarlet light fell through Drew Mallory's window and put an angry glow on one side of the colonel's face; it turned his mane of hair to flame. Ben Hannibal closed the door and stood at attention.

"At ease, Lieutenant."

The corners of Mallory's stern mouth were drawn down. His face appeared singularly cruel, half in shadow, half bloody alight. He said, "I'll be taking the regiment across the border. I intend to wipe out Togomasai's followers and burn the rancherias to the ground. We have Mexican cooperation."

When Ben Hannibal did not speak, Mallory said, "You don't appear particularly happy to hear that."

"It's very good news, sir."

"I hoped for more enthusiasm."

Mallory was looking right at him. Because of the light he could not see Mallory's eyes. Ben Hannibal waited, and Mallory said, "Someone once remarked to me that what this regiment needed was a star to follow. That's a good phrase, don't you think?"

"I suppose it is, yes, sir."

"After your showing at Weaver's Canyon I've decided that you are to be that star. We're in strange circumstances, almost at war and yet not at war. This regiment has been at peace, and now if we're going off to war, we have to suspend a few of their ideas. They need war songs and war legends. Two nights ago you made yourself a legend. The story traveled through the entire regiment within an hour of your return."

Mallory's voice dropped to a lower pitch. "Those men would follow you across the Styx, mister. I intend to foster that feeling, and I intend to have you do your part in nourishing it. I'm going to forget the fact that you deliberately opened fire on a group containing an unarmed civilian. I'm going to forget that it was no more than a witless idiot's gesture to go down that cliff after the wounded man. I don't know what prompted it—perhaps vanity or some misguided altruism, but it certainly wasn't common sense. I'm wiping those things off the record. Not because I want to favor you, understand that. I intend to put you and your troop in the forefront of every action. You'll be twice as exposed and twice as vulnerable as any other man in my command. I'm setting you up as a target. Without malice—although I believe nothing you've done deserves anything but contempt, at bottom. You behaved like a bloodthirsty fool, but as it happens, you're just the kind of fool I need right now. Do we understand each other?"

"Yes, sir."

"Good." Mallory got up. "Let's go to supper."

It was an invitation that Ben Hannibal could hardly turn down. There was no friendliness in it; it was obviously part of Mallory's method of grooming Ben Hannibal as the regimental hero. Ben Hannibal thought, gladiators were given favored treatment, too.

From the porch Ben Hannibal saw Van De Reuter walking the little dog across the compound. A thin rim of the dying sun glared on the western mountain. Mallory said abruptly, "What's that man's name?"

"Trooper Van De Reuter."

"Call him over."

Ben Hannibal called the Dutchman. Van De Reuter turned, looked at them, came obediently forward; once he stopped and bent over to cough. His feet tended to drag when he walked. He saluted. Drew Mallory said, "Is that your animal, Trooper?"

"Yes, sir."

"I understand it sleeps in the barracks," Mallory said. "I won't have that here. You'll have to find a home for him off the post or get rid of him. I don't want to see that dog on post again."

There was no change at all in Van De Reuter's rodent expression. He saluted and picked up the dog and carried it away through the main gate. The sun was all gone. Dusk came on shifting layers of twilight.

The December sky was bright. The air was cool with diamond clarity. Justin Harris left his troop to drill under the first sergeant. He was weary of drilling and watching men drill. He threw his officer's cape across his shoulders against the cold and walked into the settlement, the cape flowing behind. He stopped at the gunsmith's to collect the Smith & Wesson revolver he had ordered; the weapon was capable of ejecting all six cartridges simultaneously and therefore could be reloaded more rapidly than the issue revolvers. He had a passing thought—I suppose I should be saving my pay if I'm going to think about marriage. But when he turned into the Homestead Saloon and had that day's first look at Georgia, it recalled to him something she had said: "I don't want you to make any changes on my account. I hate reformed characters."

It was something she would not have to worry about very much. He was too much a vassal to his moods.

He saw that Ben Hannibal was with her. It irritated him a little. Georgia saw that in him; her eyes glinted, and he glared at her, resenting her amusement. He said nothing to Ben Hannibal. Two teamsters were bucking Georgia's game. Justin Harris sat down and watched the play. Small coins changed hands desultorily as the cards slipped out of the faro box. Georgia hardly glanced at the cards as she uncovered them. "Your number is seven." Ben Hannibal was watching her hands: lithe, smooth Japanese hands. It was an hour before the teamsters left. Ben Hannibal's beer had gone warm and flat; he had hardly touched it. Justin Harris spoke when the two cardplayers were gone. "What's on your mind?"

"I wanted to talk to Georgia, but I guess it's no good."

"Have you tried?"

"I've changed my mind too many times. It's no good."

"You never made up your mind," Georgia told him.

"I wanted to," Ben Hannibal said. "I suppose I didn't have the guts. I don't know what's missing in me. You two seem to understand a lot of things that just won't come out for me. Listen, you're all right. Both of you. But I won't be coming around any more." He screwed up a brief smile. "You'll just have to do without me. I guess you'll manage. *Hasta luego.*"

Ben Hannibal left the saloon, and Justin Harris said, "Christ. You'd think he was moving to Constantinople. It's a small post."

"Let him be, Justin."

"I intend to. Only—"

"Only what?"

He confessed, "I wish I could help him out of the fog."

"We'll have enough to do helping ourselves. We're neither one of us pillars." She reached for Ben Hannibal's forgotten mug of beer and drank it straight down. Afterward she made a sour face. "I think I'd like to give myself a party. Want to join me?"

Justin Harris had nothing better to do. "All right," he said.

Beth Mueller watched the desert through her window. Her shoulders were poised. "I won't take all the blame, Drew." She came around restlessly.

Mallory said, "You don't have to take any of it."

"I've been wrong. But it was you who turned me away. When things went well and you needed someone to celebrate with you, then you came to me. You don't celebrate any more, do you?"

"No."

She moved with unthinking grace across half the space between them; she put her hands on the back of an empty chair. "It was when things went badly that you shut me out. Just when I wanted to give you comfort—you gave me your back. Maybe you didn't need sympathy, but I needed to give it to you. I needed to have you accept it. For my sake."

"I'm sorry."

She said in a washed-out way, "Will you be back in time for Christmas?"

"I can't say. I'm sorry."

"Oh, stop saying, 'I'm sorry.'"

"I'm sor—" He stopped and laughed; she laughed with him, but afterward she said, "We'll be gone, at all events, when you get back." She raised her guard.

But he only turned a little way around, as if struck a light blow. "You've decided."

"Yes,"

Mallory stood near the door; he looked ready to retreat. Beth said, "John wants to write his reminiscences. He'll have that to keep him busy—he's not destroyed, at least."

"Do you have to go with him?"

"I've chosen to," she replied.

"Then I wish you both the best of luck."

She pursed her lips ironically. "Yes, of course." She was left looking down at her hands on the back of the empty chair; she looked drained. "Is that all you can say to me?"

"It seems to me we haven't had much to say to each other at all. It's my fault. I'm cut that way. Sometimes at night I wish I could bring back the past. I'm sorry, Beth."

She did not laugh. She came to him; she touched a button of his uniform and drew her index fingernail down his chest. Her

face tipped up, and he discovered that her eyes were cloudy with
tears. She stood on her toes and kissed his mouth.

"Good-bye, Drew. I've my own wishes, too. Take care in
Mexico—take care."

His head dropped. "Good-bye." He wheeled out of the house,
walking with even strides. The sunlight for a moment blinded
him. He strode along Officers' Row and down the side of the
parade ground. Enough of the turmoil within him was evident
to make Sergeant Major McCracken stiffen when he came up.
Whatever greeting had been on McCracken's lips was never
voiced. McCracken was in field uniform this morning.

Soldiers led saddled horses from the stables. The regimental
band, posted near the main gate, piped a martial tune. The air
was cool, and Mallory put on his cloak. One by one the Troops
advanced, formed into ranks and columns, facing the flagpole,
and the bugler rode ahead and sat ready in the gateway. Officers
took their positions. Ben Hannibal led the first Troop. Pete
Rubio rode around a corner into the compound, slouching on
the back of an ugly squat horse. The quartermaster and the
sutler stood together under a porch roof. Women stood around;
children watched. The home-guard reserve troops stood afoot
in formation at the back corner of the quadrangle.

The regimental colors rode forward. McCracken waddled
around the headquarters office to bring out the colonel's horse,
after which McCracken mounted with a heave and a wheeze
and trotted to the head of the column to take a position immediately behind Captain McQuestion, who was acting as the
colonel's aide. The wagon train formed up outside the post.

The ground was very dry. The quartermaster had a word with
the sutler and went outside to talk with the wagon drivers. Dust
stirred around the horses. Drew Mallory leveled his hat and put
a foot in the stirrup. He stepped up and rode diagonally across
the parade ground to a post in front of Captain McQuestion.
Mallory's studious glance traveled down the line and paused on
Ben Hannibal. Hannibal stared back, his face gray and dusty.

Mallory could see down the length of Officers' Row. Just past
his own house was Mueller's. Mueller was on the porch in a
wheelchair. Mallory could not make out his face at this
distance. It struck him that he had known Mueller for a good
many years. Mueller remained an empty face in his mind. He

had only the most superficial impressions of what might have been Mueller's dreams and beliefs and loves and losses.

Beth stood at the white picket gate. When she saw Mallory turn, she lifted her hand to shoulder height in a hesitant signal. Mallory wondered what would become of her. He made no acknowledgment of her gesture. He knew he would not see her again. He wished he could bring back the sharp edges of emotions that had been warm, but his face remained cool; he saw her only at a distance. He had the vague hope that Mueller would not wash all the color from her by keeping her out of the light. Mallory suspected she would find another man to serve her needs while she waited upon Mueller not as a wife but as a caretaker. Mallory thought, I would like to have kept her, but it was only a gentle wish, without force. It had not been any code that had kept him from her. He had been unable to rouse whatever passions might have lain dormant inside himself. The years had encrusted him with layers of unfeelingness. Perhaps at first it had been a façade, a manifestation of the deliberate character he believed an officer should present. But it had gripped him too tightly, and he knew, without much regret, that it had destroyed a large part of him; he was not right inside—he knew it—and yet the very nature of his loss made it impossible for him to lament.

His face hardened. He had a glimpse of Justin Harris, back along the line, leaning down in the saddle to talk with a woman who had run up to speak with him and take his hand. The woman, Mallory saw, was the same woman who was to have married Ben Hannibal. It puzzled Mallory momentarily. He turned straight ahead, raised his hand overhead, and spoke.

"Column of fours." He dropped his hand smartly forward.

The plan was worked out with care. The regiment rode southeast toward Lordsburg: it was Mallory's plan to make it appear that the regiment was going away, to the East, for the winter. They reached Fort Bowie, and on the succeeding five days patrols of various strengths rode from Fort Bowie in every direction. The patrols crossed the border into Mexico singly, sometimes by night, riding by devious routes toward a rendezvous in a massive hidden gully protected by cottonwoods. The cottonwood leaves were yellow and brown and red; with the first drop in temperature they would fall to the ground.

The regiment gathered silently, and then it waited. Men and horses grew impatient and short-tempered. Mallory was waiting for a change in the weather that would cover their movements. The days dragged. Agency scouts filed in and out of the camp like streams of ants, keeping tabs on the trails, the weather, and the dark hatchet summits of the great Sierra immediately to the south. Three Mimbreño warriors caught in the vicinity were gagged and bound to trees along Justin Harris's company street, to prevent their carrying word to Togomasai in the mountains. A Yaqui scout came in, riding a mule, and after a monosyllabic talk with the Yaqui, Pete Rubio reported that the three Apache rancherias in the Sierra were settling down for winter. Heavy clouds rolled up from the west. Drew Mallory watched the sky and gave orders for two hours' dismounted close-order drill.

## 11

A listless rain fell upon the mountains. In the narrow canyons hung a stinging chill and a musty, lifeless smell—like catacombs, like a mausoleum. Black rocks glistened. There was a thick shine on the flapping oilskin ponchos. The faces of the men were gray like the rain; no one spoke.

Serpentine, the regiment climbed with slow weariness, horses and men moving at a grim and plodding pace. Here and there a corpse-hued face turned upward to scan the scarps and cliffs, cut by slashing blades of rain, but most of the faces hung tucked and bowed under hatbrims from which streams of water ran, as if from drain spouts.

The earth pitched upward, tortured and uneven; it climbed

endlessly, as if it stubbornly sought heaven—its end lay out of sight in the gloom. Fragments of light raced down the folds of the wide, dark slickers, coiling about the men: funeral robes, black wings, sepulchral capes. Soldiers in wet, tired misery.

Spread loose along the bends, the column was more than half a mile long. At the head Drew Mallory walked with sturdy strides, leading his horse. His head was lifted: he did not blink when raindrops struck his face.

He was set and fixed: there was nothing malleable about him. The face of Drew Mallory was all crags and gaunt hollows, cruel, closed. His eyes were pitted into deep, narrowed sockets, and even the rain did not dim his white hair.

He spoke over his shoulder. "Mount."

Softly the command passed back from man to man, carried on voices edged with the hoarseness of exhaustion. One by one, the weary, dark figures hauled themselves onto the split-fork saddles. The line did not stop.

Ben Hannibal passed the command on and mounted his horse. He tucked his slicker down around his knees and saw, some distance behind him, Justin Harris's studied glance. Harris was visible for a brief interval while the column single-filed a slow bend. Harris showed a quick, wan smile. Ben Hannibal nodded in reply; he had no smile to return. He had the feeling that a banner flew from the peak of his hat crown, and when he looked back again, he found the troop sergeant's eyes flat on him. He heard himself speak. "Tired, Bodeen?"

"Not specially, sir," the huge sergeant said. Ben Hannibal knew he was lying. No man in the regiment wasn't tired; in rump and blistered feet, in eyes strained raw and rein-calloused hands, in saddle-rubbed knees, tired in jarred bones after a night and a day and another soaking night climbing, pitching, moving. They punished themselves beyond their limits and kept right on because Drew Mallory was indefatigable and his brittle, hooded eyes challenged them without mercy, and there was not a man willing to give in to him.

Ben Hannibal said, "It won't be too long, Bodeen."

"Yes, sir," Bodeen said, without confidence. Bodeen's big hips spilled over the sides of the saddle. He dwarfed his horse, but he was not fat.

Ben Hannibal did not think about the snow-buried misery

waiting at the top. He was not certain any more that there was a top. It was a summitless mountain, an infinite climb; they would crawl upward forever through the cold rain and clinging mud. It was no use trying to climb out of hell.

Arms, legs, heads, souls, horses. The regiment made a reluctant turn to squeeze through a thin rock chimney. Rivulets matted the clay and made soft, unsafe footing. The slate rain threatened to turn to snow; the temperature hung just on the verge. Damp cold air and the drizzle muffled all sound of travel. In the steep canyon the horses had to slog up through hock-deep mud that sucked at their fetlocks like an unweaned calf at its mother's teat.

In the ugly duckling troop Ben Hannibal's troopers rode slouched and indifferent. Here, in the blind bowels of the regiment, one man—Trooper Hans De Reuter—sat perched like a drowned sparrow on the back of his bony horse. It plunged him forward and back, an ungainly beast, the worst-gaited horse in the regiment. Van De Reuter's wasted little body clung to it, and no one knew where his strength came from; he was dying, and everyone knew he was dying. A hum of rain-softened talk droned around him, but none of it appeared to touch Van De Reuter's consciousness. The eyes, lifeless, did not move in his parchment face.

Corporal Blockman was talking. His voice was an unhappy twang. "Six days we sit in that puking gully, and then it rains and the bastard moves us out."

"Son-of-a-bitch," someone said numbly.

Corporal Blockman said, "It was August he'd march us across the puking desert, but Christmastime and he figures we about due for a blizzard, so he drive us up here. Puking God-damned Sierra." His voice trailed off, an ineffectual bleating in the wilderness.

Trooper Hoag said, "The old Rock done fixed it all up for us, a nice tidy little blizzard."

"Just to keep us fit," said Corporal Blockman. No one laughed.

Bodeen's voice, disembodied, came from ahead. "Save your energy back there, now."

For a while no one talked. Trooper Van De Reuter bent forward on the lurching horse. He seemed to be fighting nausea.

Presently he ripped up a ragged, painful cough. They crossed a barren rock shelf and threaded a stand of pines half-drowned in rainfall. A floor of conifer needles floated deceptively on the waterlogged earth. Footing was even worse than before. Corporal Blockman huddled his ungainly bulk inside the slicker; his eyes burned like those of a drunk.

Trooper Hoag said, "Hell, we ain't about to find nothing in this muck. Ain't no Apache stupid enough to show hisself for a fight in this kind of soup. What the hell we doing here, anyways?"

"We just getting exercise," Blockman told him.

Hoag said. "What the old man don't know about Indian fighting you could fill up Cooke's *Manual* with."

"That's for damned puking certain. Old man got my puking brother killed, just such a fool play as this—and they were no need for it, no need at all, now."

"He's a God-damned butcher," said Trooper Hoag anxiously.

"Tooken my brother and sixty good puking men out after Comanche on the God-damned-your-ass Llano Estacado," Boone Blockman began, and then Bodeen's voice hurtled back.

"We heard plenty of times about your brother, Corp. Let's have it quiet back there."

Trooper Van De Reuter arched over a spasm of harsh coughs. They seemed to rend his throat. After that the only sounds were the squelch of hoofs and an occasional muted jingle of bit chains. Ben Hannibal rode with the echo of the troopers' talk riding around inside the cavern of his skull.

McCracken glanced back. There were heads tipped forward, bobbing, men asleep in the saddle. The sergeant major had before him the shimmering T-shouldered silhouette of the colonel, the Old Man, the Rock. McCracken might have been all his life riding behind that block of unbending shadow, going uphill in a blinding gray rain with the temperature inching down steadily.

The regiment humped over a lip of rock, seeming to pause there for strength as each rider passed. It turned across the spine of a narrow ridge into a fissure between rotten limestone cliffs. The walls tipped back, went up, and disappeared in black-bottom cloud. An unseen lightning bolt sizzled, on its heels a roll of thunder. Echoes rocked back and forth down the chasm. By sunlight the broken cliffs would be yellow, red, violet, indigo. The downpour blotted them into nondescript monochrome.

A vague squat rider came down to meet them, a brown man on a compact horse who swung in and rode at Mallory's shoulder. There was a brief conversation, too soft to reach McCracken. The Indian scout urged his horse ahead into the gloom, and McCracken, who seldom missed much, saw the colonel's shoulders settle.

Mallory beckoned to him. McCracken rode ahead, and the colonel said, "Dispatch a man back to Captain Kapsimahlis. Tell him to post flankers as soon as we break out of this canyon. Four to each flank, half a mile out, provisioned. And drop the rear guard back to five hundred yards with one of the Agency scouts to ride half a mile behind that."

"Indians, Colonel?"

"Just obey your orders, Sergeant Major."

"Yes, sir."

McCracken fell back, passed Ben Hannibal, and chose a trooper. He sent the trooper back along the line with the colonel's orders. McCracken tried to shift his seat on the saddle, but there was no comfort left anywhere on his expanse of raw flesh. He settled stolid in the rack and saw that Ben Hannibal was smoking a cigarette under his lowered hatbrim. McCracken resumed his place in line behind the colonel and brooded upon Mallory's enigmatic back.

Today, McCracken thought, today is Christmas Eve. He worked his big stem-winder out from beneath the poncho and snapped open its lid, sheltering the face with his hand. Seven-fifty. He put the watch away in his pocket. It might as well have been noon or sundown or midnight. Time of day was meaningless. McCracken's eyelids were heavy, slitted against the rain. A frigid wind sluiced down the gorge, cut through his clothes, drove needle-pointed droplets directly into his florid face. His blistered feet filled the waterlogged boots to capacity, and he knew he dared never remove the boots until they dried, or they would shrink and he would never get them on again. He slipped a hand under his oilskin and rubbed his paunch and believed it had diminished remarkably in the past thirty-six hours.

He looked upward at the cliffs and observed that it was a likely spot for a trap. Colonel Mallory said, "Dismount and lead," and stepped down into the muck as though it were a dry raked parade ground.

McCracken passed the word and swung his leg over, dropped gingerly to the soles of his feet, and listened abstractedly to the squeeze and squish of water in the boots.

In places he had to use his hands to climb. The canyon was that steep. Once, raising his head, he saw the colonel looking back at him. Whatever was in Mallory's expression, it was not pity or concern. McCracken tried to put on a smile. He puffed and said, "A fat man sure carries a cross, don't he?" The colonel turned away and kept on going up the crevasses without smiling, without answering. McCracken wondered where Mallory's infinite endurance came from. He knew every man in the regiment hated the colonel today, and he thought suddenly, he wants us to hate him.

Exactly on the hour by his snap-lid pocket timepiece, McCracken spoke ahead through the rain. "Time, sir."

"All right," Mallory said. His hand lifted in signal.

McCracken turned. "Five minutes. Close up and rest. No smokes. Pass the word."

A voice from down the line reached him faintly. "Jesus, nobody can see ten feet in this God-damned weather. No smokes, and my belly's growling."

"Close up. Five-minute halt." The word passed, softly. "No smokes. Pass it on." Men settled one by one, links in a chain falling over. Men sat on rocks by the trail, or in the mud itself, or stood with an arm hooked over saddles because they knew if they sat down they would be too tired to get up.

Trooper Hans Van De Reuter stayed seated on his saddle. He was slumped over and coughed now and then. Trooper Hoag's dull, curiously high voice called through the rain, "Happy Christmas, boys."

"Ain't Christmas yet," growled Boone Blockman. "Puking God-damned army."

Hoag had a nervous laugh. "All right, then, happy Christmas Eve."

Corporal Blockman said, "Old man's saving us up a blizzard we can celebrate Christmas with, proper. A blizzard and hardtack, blisters and saddle sores and maybe some frost-bite. No Injuns, though." He tipped his square head back to squint ahead. "Long road," he said. "Long puking road. I wish we had Van De Reuter's puking dog along. Even that scrawny meat'd taste good about now."

A reflection glowed briefly in Van De Reuter's clouded eyes. "Shut up about my dog." He was not looking at Blockman.

Trooper Hoag said, "Van De Reuter, you all right?" And getting no answer, did not pursue the inquiry.

Justin Harris walked forward along the side of the rail, idly touching a bridle bit here and a cinch there. At the head of the troop Ben Hannibal stood with his back to a tree. His hat was low across his face. He kept his chilled hands inside the folds of his slicker. Justin Harris came up with a commonplace greeting. Ben Hannibal caught a young trooper staring at him from ten yards away; Ben Hannibal turned angry and said to Harris, "See that?"

"What?"

"Trooper Crane."

"He looks all right to me," Harris said.

"He hasn't taken his eyes off me."

"You've got to expect a little of that, Ben."

"I'm sick of it, if you want to know. I wish they'd find something else to stare at."

"If that was all we had to worry about," Harris said. "Take it easy, Ben. They won't hurt you."

"I think they expect me to choose out Togomasai and duel him single-handed—and then take on his whole bunch by myself."

"Maybe they do. I wouldn't fret about it. It's what the colonel wants."

"To hell with the God-damned colonel." Ben Hannibal lifted one leg and placed the foot, toe-down, against the tree. "To hell with the old man. You ever see a man walk a high wire, Justin? People don't watch him just to admire his God-damned balance. They don't respect him for his courage or judgment. They just wait for him to fall off."

"Well, you haven't got anything to fall off of, outside of your horse."

"Christ, you know what I mean."

Harris's rawboned shoulders moved under the dripping oilskin. He rubbed his hands together. "Why talk about it?"

"All right," Ben Hannibal said. He tipped his face down on his chest.

Justin Harris moved away a few paces. He was loose, slack-jointed, exhausted. He looked down the line. In the half obscurity he saw one figure still asaddle: Van De Reuter. Trooper Hoag was standing by Van De Reuter's stirrup, talking, evidently getting no reply. Justin Harris thought, we should have left Van De Reuter behind last night when he started to spit blood. But there was nobody to leave with him, and alone in the cold rain Van De Reuter would have died, anyway.

Van De Reuter's lungs were undoubtedly ruptured. "He's dead now," the surgeon had said, coming away from him. Van De Reuter was dying, but at least he had company—although he gave no sign that he knew it or cared. Harris left him alone. He had seen consumptives reach a stage before. Sometimes they went off in the head. There was nothing anybody could do for Van De Reuter, and Justin Harris walked back to his horse in time for the remount call.

Abruptly the chill rain quit.

It held off during a crystal hour while the temperature plummeted. Precisely at two o'clock by the sergeant major's watch the regiment made a halt on a wide rock shelf overhung by mountain towers of weather-blasted granite. Drew Mallory, with breath steaming out of his nostrils, gathered his oilskin slicker into precise folds and tied it neatly across the cantle of his polished and rain-spattered saddle. After that, and without the appearance of hurry, he unfolded a crude map and bent over it with Pete Rubio. Rubio spoke in short bursts which were inaudible six feet away. McCracken listened impassively, heard very little, and kept most of his attention on the grim, threatening sky and the face of his watch. In two minutes the colonel straightened and spoke.

"Sergeant Major."

"Sir."

"Troop commanders. On the double."

"Sir," McCracken responded smartly. He swung to dispatch a rider.

The air hung brittle and clear underneath an advancing blanket of heavier cloud. It unrolled from the northwest. For the first time in twenty hours the rear was visible from the head of the column. Captains and lieutenants cantered up and dismounted. Back along the line the voices that had complained of the rain and fog now reviled the visibility. "Suppose they's a Mimbreño up one of yonder rocks. Just one Apache, all it takes to settle our scalp."

"Rubio and the scouts supposed to've cleared out the rocks."

"What odds you give they ain't overlooked one bright-eyed redskin in the rain, all them rocks?"

"No odds at all, Billy Joe, no odds at all. Just the same, I wouldn't expect to stay hid long if Rubio was bound and determined to root me out. I seen him on a bet pick one set of pony tracks out of the main street in Spanish Flat and follow it right to the stable stall. He could track a fly across your ugly face."

"He's just one man. Only so much ground one man can cover —and only take one bullet to cut him out. You expect Pete Rubio's eyes to keep your hide safe, you go right ahead. Me, I keep my carbine loaded, orders or no orders. We strung out along here like a school of salmon waiting for a net."

"I don't know, I figure the old man knows where he's at."

"Sure. Only I wish I knowed what he got in his head. Getting cold as a witch's tit. Four hours to dark, if a blizzard don't hit before then. I ain't never going to cuss the desert sun again. And what I want to know, when we going to get some sleep? I got grindstones in both eyes."

At the head of his troop, Lt. Will Sandin tired of listening to them. "Settle down, soldiers." He left his horse's reins trailing and walked back along the column. "Better tighten those blanket straps, Cohan."

"Yes, sir."

"You feeling all right?"

"I'd be a liar if I said yes, Lieutenant."

"All marches reach an end, Cohan. Just keep plugging. Mind that horse—it may mean your life."

"I will, sir."

Sandin could see Ben Hannibal down the line. Hannibal had his shoulder propped against the rock wall and his arms folded;

he looked angry. The gray air made him look gaunt and wretched. Sandin's attention shifted absently to the little cadre of captains and scouts still knotted around Colonel Mallory, far up the rock shelf. The sky was a sullied blanket; the cliffs glistened. The captains came riding back. Sandin said to his sergeant, "Time to mount up."

The black rank of heavy clouds marched steadily across. Pete Rubio rode away from them into the mountain shadows while the regiment strung itself out and moved. The cursing of troopers was weak and despondently weary. Drew Mallory rode alertly, with eyes set deep in their sockets, a man of sinuous strength with an arrogant jaw and a back so erect it seemed corseted.

Time crawled through the long gray afternoon. Men slept asaddle, in snatches. The regiment messed on dry cold food washed down with a canteen ration, then mounted and advanced to the higher crags of the Sierra, moving like an antique train in need of oiling. Trooper Van De Reuter clung to his saddle by an incredible display of will. Trooper Hoag's hoarse voice and Corporal Blockman's had gone silent. Even Justin Harris fought the weight of raw, heavy lids and pounded bones. A total stillness held the cold air in pockets so breathless they deadened the sound of progress. An Agency scout appeared on horseback at a mountain saddle half a mile away, raised a hand in signal, and swept off the skyline.

The regiment curled over the pulley of a narrow pass and slithered through an open meadow of rocks. A rider came trotting back along the line to gather officers and send them forward. The sky was gray up to a midpoint and darker beyond that; the blackest clouds moved up like artillery batteries, rolling into position with tall, misty lances breaking from their crests. The captains and lieutenants came around the colonel. That was when Pete Rubio, as though a whisper had reached out to him across the peaks, came riding down to the conference.

Mallory said, "Well, Chief of Scouts?"

"It'll blow," Rubio said. "Good and hard. Maybe a half hour from now, no more. No birds in sight—everything's gone down to lower ground."

Captain McQuestion said, "What's our altitude?"

"Maybe eight thousand foot."

McQuestion asked, "What are our chances of getting snowed under?"

"Pretty good," Rubio said dispassionately. "You going to get a norther now. High wind could blow a man and horse right off this mountain. We ain't careful, we be scattered sixty miles time it blows over."

Mallory rode with his mouth's cruel corners turned down and did not speak. Rubio added, "Drifts going to run fifteen, twenty foot deep in the hollows after the blow. Going to be a chore to find a way through."

Mallory said abruptly, "Have you ever been lost, Rubio?"

"No, sir."

"All right."

Will Sandin said, "How long will the storm last?"

"Till she gets tired. Ain't no telling. Six hours, maybe six days."

Justin Harris rode along at the fringe of the group with Ben Hannibal, chewing an unlit cigar and listening to the talk while his eyes swept the cliffs. Mallory said, "Togomasai is still in his rancherias."

"Yes, sir. He wanted to pull out for low ground a week back, but he's got a bunch of wounded as can't travel yet, 'count of Lieutenant Hannibal's scrap with them."

Will Sandin said, "How did you learn that, Pete?"

"I got ears."

Justin Harris said, "We'd better find a spot to button up."

Colonel Mallory swiveled in the saddle. His head swung in a slow arc. "We need high ground but out of the wind. I think we'll dig in on the south slope of the mountain. Any other suggestions?"

It was Justin Harris who spoke. "Does that make a change in our plans, Colonel?"

"Only in the timing. We'll break out of here as soon as the weather allows. You can be assured the Apaches won't be going anywhere in the meantime. How far from here, Chief of Scouts?"

"Six, seven miles. That could be a full day's ride in deep snow."

Captain McQuestion said, "If the norther lasts more than two days, we won't have enough rations for men or horses."

"We'll make do," Mallory said.

"How?"

"Captain, do you want to record that you wish to turn back?"

"No, sir."

Justin Harris kept silent. Mallory glanced at him as if expecting him to speak. Harris was watching McQuestion. McQuestion was bowlegged and solid, skin the color and texture of old cowhide. He had come up from the ranks; he was forty-six and much more cautious than he had been during the war, when he had earned his commission in the field.

Mallory said, "Picket the horses on short hobbles in those firs near the base of the mountain. Horse guards to be changed every half hour—Lieutenant Sandin's troop will supply the men for that. String your men among the rocks. Each man to find the best shelter and roll up by twos inside blankets and ponchos. I'll post myself above that rock chimney. When you're dug in, take your bearings carefully. You won't be able to see once the wind comes up. Lieutenant Hannibal, I'll want your troop posted up at the perimeter on the long chance we're spotted by Mimbreño scouts."

Justin Harris said, "That's a little rough."

Mallory said tightly, "Confine your mouth, Captain." He looked around. "That's all. Report to me when you're secured."

McCraken came up, and Mallory uttered a quiet command. McCracken wheeled his horse back, bellowing, "Dismount and lead—dismount and lead." A groan ran the length of the column.

Ben Hannibal took his orders from the colonel without any observable reaction. He deployed his thirty-six men along an arc of boulders at the crest of the hill. They would be murderously exposed. He talked to them with more assurance than he felt.

"Dig in on the downwind side or you'll be drifted under. The steeper the ground the better. Double your blankets, wrap in ponchos by twos—don't even stick your noses out once the storm comes. On the run, now."

Bodeen went after them like a sheep dog worrying its flock. Ben Hannibal saw the sky boiling with black violence. Men carrying slickers and blankets moved across the mountain like bats in the half light. He heard the chipping of hand shovels against the flinty mountainside. He memorized a path that would take him rock by rock past Harris's position down to the colonel's. Pete Rubio was down there, conferring with Mallory under a high granite spire.

Clayton, the surgeon, came along with his kit, anxiously watching the sky. He said to Ben Hannibal, "Make sure they wrap up tight, and see you do the same yourself. I'm not equipped to handle cases of frostbite and exposure."

"All right," Ben Hannibal said. "Will you have another look at Van De Reuter?"

"Not that it will do any good." The surgeon picked a path away through the rocks. A single flake of snow touched Ben Hannibal's cheek, and he slapped at it angrily as though it were a mosquito.

In a little while the surgeon returned. "The man's a fool. He ought to be in a sanitarium. He refused laudanum— he must be in indescribable pain. I don't see what keeps him going, or what would make him want to try. He's utterly rotted away inside."

"Well," Ben Hannibal said, "thanks just the same."

"I've never been able to understand the various ways people react to suffering," the surgeon said. He walked away, swinging his kit.

Ben Hannibal stared across the still earth. His collar was turned up; a breath of wind flapped it against his jaw; then the air settled into unsettling motionlessness. Sergeant Bodeen climbed up to him. Bodeen stumbled once or twice. "All dug in, sir."

Ben Hannibal frowned at him. The big sergeant was all but out on his feet. "All right, Bodeen. Let's have a look."

He went from boulder to boulder, inspecting his men. They were like moles preparing for hibernation. He said, "Where are your rations, McVey?"

"I put them somewheres around here, sir." The trooper's teeth were rattling.

"Take them inside with you."

"Holy Jesus, Lieutenant—we going to be here that long?"

"Maybe," Ben Hannibal said. He moved on. Bodeen, at

his shoulder, tripped and caught himself and stopped with a drunken, puzzled expression. "What's that noise?"

Ben Hannibal turned his head and caught it on the flats of his eardrums, a distant moan. "That's the wind," he said. "Hello, Crane. All tucked in?"

"Yes, sir."

"When the snow comes, pull that flap down over your head. Keep your blanket propped up or you won't have enough air to breathe."

"Yes, sir."

"You'll be all right. Just get some sleep. You've been wanting a chance to do that, haven't you?"

Crane swallowed and stared at him. Ben Hannibal said, "Who's sharing the blankets with you?"

"I am, Lieutenant," said Bodeen. When they walked out of Trooper Crane's hearing, the sergeant said, "Kid's tied up in granny knots. Figured I'd best stay with him. Seems his daddy froze to death in Donner Pass. He's scared half to puking."

"Funny he didn't say anything."

"He don't want to let it show. Any other officer, maybe he would. But he don't want *you* to think he's scared."

"Hell, we're all scared, Bodeen."

"Not me. I'm just too damned tired to care."

They reached a steep pitch beneath a rock slab. Two men in their hollowed cocoon: Trooper Hoag and Cpl. Boone Blockman. Blockman was snoring sonorously. Ben Hannibal said, "Think you can sleep through that racket, Hoag?"

"I ain't bothered about that. Lieutenant, sir, you figure we going to pull through?"

"No question of it," Ben Hannibal said. "Kick him if he keeps you awake."

"No, sir. Long as I can hear him sawing, I know I'm all right."

Ben Hannibal started to move on, but Hoag's voice stopped him. "Lieutenant."

"Yes?"

"I wish you could've had a better Christmas."

"Why, thanks, Hoag."

They walked on, and Bodeen said, "That's a spooky wind.

Louder all the time, but you still can't feel it. Christ, it's cold."

"Go on back and turn in, Bodeen."

"Thanks, Lieutenant. I will. And listen, about Christmas, and what Hoag said, I—"

"It's not Christmas till tomorrow, Bodeen, and maybe the sun will shine."

"Yes, sir." The giant sergeant turned back, walking with blind weariness. Bodeen had stood sentry duty for two weaker men and had not slept in four nights.

When Ben Hannibal reached the end of the line, he tucked in the last of his men and went back to his rock-sheltered post. He lay engulfed in folded thicknesses of blankets and oilskins. The air was without movement, but the wind cried. He pushed his rations and hat down inside the bedroll with him. The tip of his nose was numb. He rubbed it with his palm and lifted his head to look down the hill. He saw Mallory standing rock-still, legs braced against the uneven ground, only his head moving in a slow arc. The moan of the wind rose in pitch. Out of the head of the rushing clouds, smoky spirals shot downward. A thin snowfall began, delicate and gentle. Ben Hannibal shifted his holster around to a more comfortable position. He reminded himself to wiggle his toes at intervals.

## 12

The great storm came across the mountains. Not all at once, but in a steady rise of wind, the dry rustle of stirring dead things, a stately march of blackness. Behind the first rank of cloud, a crisp fall of snowflakes. The whimper of the wind, rising to a shriek but yet muffled by the vacuum of calm air— distant, like the call of a sailor on the mast of a far ship. And on the hillside, exposed like naked embryos, the rolled shapes of men.

A single antelope, with no business at this altitude, sprang hopelessly across the hilltop and bounded downhill, running before the storm. On its rump the signal spots of alarm flashed white, bobbed, and went out of sight.

The hill blinded men to the advance of the storm. The blast hit them abruptly. Below, in the trees, the horse guards gathered their blankets tight and used yellow bandannas to tie their hats down around their ears, and because their faces were exposed to the norther, they were the first to experience the extraordinary petrifying force of its knives. They turned their backs to it and bowed, braced against thick trees, and counted time, second by second, awaiting their relief.

The air blasted, near freezing; as the furious wind smashed through, the deadly effect of the cold became savage. Snow whipped the mountains like rawhide lashes. The occasional hailstone had the velocity of a bullet. This gray afternoon turned to a swirl of black-and-white gloom and then to a violent obscurity that had no color. In it a man, even if he could force his eyes open, saw nothing. The song of the norther was a moan, a roar, a cry, finally a scream of terror; it never paused for breath.

In a man's ear it came through ponchos and blankets like the wail of a locomotive whistle six inches away. Troopers endured the storm, proud of their whipcord bodies; the storm was the fist of Drew Mallory, and men resisted it gamely.

Snow swept down the mountainside in great sheets, piled high in the hollows and then blew away on gusts. The turmoil was so deafening it became an unbearable monotony. It whipped through the canyons and stripped pines bare of needles. No one knew when it would end.

Hans Van De Reuter was all wrapped up in his layers of poncho and blanket, but just the same the cold reached inside and felt like heat searing his cheeks. Sprays and columns of snow-smoke wheeled down the hill; the noise smashed, recoiled, smashed. Van De Reuter felt a spasm coming on. He drew his knees up to his chin and began to cough, his eyes wide open in the blackness.

The sticky taste of his life came up through his windpipe; it lay thick on his tongue. The half-articulate certainty of death reached him faintly; it was in the flicker and fade of his sensations.

In a sudden pocket of the storm he thought he heard the high-pitched barking of a dog.

The blizzard roared through the afternoon and, without darkening, into the night. Van De Reuter doubled himself and lay glossy, half awake. The stink of blood mingled with bad air in this tiny confinement. In the pit of his chest a hard knot of pain swelled. He dropped a lump of half-congealed thickness from his mouth. It fell on the back of his hand and stuck. His body shook from time to time; after a tremor he would fall limp, his eyes closing, exhausted; he fought them open.

All over the mountain ran the howling, incessant wind. The darkness pulsed, and little points of red light appeared before Van De Reuter, brightening when he coughed. He pushed a hole through the end of his cocoon, and the ice-cold air blasted through. It tore back a corner of his slicker and flapped it violently against his head. He pushed it away; his hand had lost all feeling. His hat swam away.

The dog was barking steadily. It was hungry. Van De Reuter rose and threw off his blankets. When he was upright, the wind struck him on the chest and knocked him flat. He crawled around, sluggishly searching. The wind made a sail of his coat and tugged him several yards down the hill. He had no gloves, and his hands were utterly without sensation. There was a taste of salt on his tongue. The dog yelped insistently somewhere ahead.

The blizzard weaving about him nailed him flat to the ground. He moved with elbows and toes; he inched forward blindly because he was too weak to rise. The snow had no depth on the ground. The wind kept it in motion. He could not breathe; he tucked his face into his shoulder to get air and began to cough. There were blades of needle-tipped pain, and then there was an explosion within him. The pain faded away. His shoulder rammed a rock. He crawled, listening to the bark of the little dog.

The driving mass of whirling snow swept across Trooper

Crane in his blankets. Beside him was the warmth of big Bodeen. He heard Bodeen's slow sleep-breathing now and then when a hollow dulled the cry of the wind. Crane's eyes were open, though he saw nothing. At intervals he opened the wrappings a tiny crack to admit air; he had a fear of suffocation. It took all his strength to keep the oilskins from flying away when he opened up. He had no idea of the hour, but he became convinced days had passed. The certainty was so strong that he ate four meals out of his rations as time passed.

A heaviness began in his bladder. He tried to put it from his mind, but an hour came when he could no longer ignore it. The need to relieve himself became a low, thick pain. It preyed on his concentration, fed his fear of freezing to death.

He wished he had deserted months ago when he had wanted to.

Bodeen stirred in his sleep. Trooper Crane held his breath. He wanted Bodeen to wake up; he wanted Bodeen to reassure him. But Bodeen only began to snore very softly. The pressure on Crane's bladder made him draw up his knees. The howling wind flapped the blanket around his head and shoulder. He pinched his cheek; it tingled and burned.

He had an image of himself, blue and frosted, frozen into brittle immovability. He shuddered; goose-bumps lifted on his flesh. The pain in his loins increased and became insistent.

He thought of Lieutenant Hannibal. His mind built the image of Lieutenant Hannibal walking down the canyon hillside, angrily shouting them on, walking into the teeth of stabbing rifle fire. Lieutenant Hannibal stopping in the midst of the fusillade, shaming Crane and the others into following him. Lieutenant Hannibal silhouetted against the flashes of rifle flame, Lieutenant Hannibal scooping Crane up, carrying him on one foot through the swirl of battle, Lieutenant Hannibal scorning a sniper's rifle to rally down the face of the cliff and bring a man to safety.

Crane's jaw crept forward, and his eyes narrowed in imitation of Lieutenant Hannibal's sun squint. The wind whipped around in frenzy. Trooper Crane chattered with cold and the pressure of his shameful pain.

He wrapped himself up and climbed out of the shelter.

The wind bent him over. The freezing blast of air sliced

wickedly, and he put his back to it. He relieved himself. It seemed to take a very long time, and he was convinced he would freeze, but then he finished and crawled back into the blankets and trembled uncontrollably.

Bodeen growled drowsily, "What the hell?" and immediately went back to sleep. Trooper Crane smiled in the dark. He felt strong, he felt vindicated, like a man who has met a great challenge. He tucked his cold hands into his armpits for warmth and closed his eyes.

The storm howled through the night with savagery that did not diminish; it broke, startlingly, in the middle of the morning, Christmas Day, and it left behind only a middling cold breeze that gathered the loose snow in drifts. The astonished regiment pawed upward, digging out. Snow lay in a glare across the slopes. Below, in the hollows, it was drifted yards deep, sometimes to the treetops. Justin Harris's horse guards found that most of the horses somehow had survived it, all but a few which had broken hobbles and probably run forty miles with the storm, or dropped over cliffs unseen in the wheel of snow.

Ben Hannibal gathered his troop in one place and said to them, "Break out your rations. Eat and run around to get warmed up. No fires."

Boone Blockman roared, "No fires? Jesus Christ, you must be—"

"Shut up," Ben Hannibal said, showing his teeth. The troopers gathered close together for warmth and ate on their feet, shifting from boot to boot. They ate snow, for the water in their canteens had frozen and, in some cases, burst the metal seams. They trembled in violent concert.

It was Ben Hannibal, tramping through the snow to report to the colonel, who found Van De Reuter.

All he found at first was Van De Reuter's boot; he tripped over it and sprawled. When he looked back, ready to curse the ground, he saw the boot; he scrambled around on hands and knees and began to bat the snow away with his hands. He gathered a small audience; the surgeon came by, Justin Harris and Lieutenant Sandin came by. They stood watching with their faces in a blank suspension.

The snow around Van De Reuter's head was stained dark.

Blood from his lips had frozen into crimson ice. His face was shrunken and white, most of it glazed with slivers of brittle ice. The eyes were open and one hand outstretched. Ben Hannibal looked uphill and then down. It was Will Sandin who spoke first. "He was on his way to the colonel."

Justin Harris said, "What do you mean?"

"He's halfway from his camp to the colonel's post. Remember the colonel made him take his dog off the post? Van De Reuter hated him for that."

The surgeon observed, "I've said it before, but it bears repeating. It's a miracle he got this far."

Sandin said, "Hate kept him alive. He wanted to kill the colonel."

Ben Hannibal said, "On account of the dog? I don't think so."

"Then what's he doing here?"

The surgeon said, "That's something we'll never know."

Ben Hannibal went away, dragging his feet. Behind him the size of the crowd around Van De Reuter increased. Ben Hannibal walked down to the rock spire and found Mallory brushing himself off. He made a report of his troop and told Mallory, "Van De Reuter's dead up there. Lieutenant Sandin thinks Van De Reuter wanted to kill you because of the dog."

Mallory said, "Bury him," and walked away.

Sergeants marched the troops around to limber them up. Pete Rubio rode out with a contingent of Agency scouts. As they left the slope, they separated to thread the mountains and penetrate the Apache stronghold singly. Drew Mallory called a meeting of officers. He said, "With any luck at all we'll take them completely by surprise." Ben Hannibal watched him; had Van De Reuter's act meant nothing to Mallory? But perhaps Sandin had been wrong. Sandin was inclined to attribute to others some of his own jealous hatred of Mallory.

Mallory said, "Mr. Hannibal, you will take the lead position with your troop. Get your men mounted. We'll meet the Chief of Scouts below that peak." His arm swept up, pointing across the lower summits to the gray pinnacle of a mountain to the southeast. A low cold wind rushed steadily across the earth flanks, stirring the surface of the snow.

Mallory said, "Captain McQuestion, call for half a dozen volunteers to break trail. None of them from Lieutenant Hannibal's troop. I want it intact. We'll travel in a column of twos, and I want it kept dressed up tight as possible. Flankers to ride in two sets, at three hundred yards and at half a mile. Captain Kapsimahlis, you'll provide the flankers from your troop, and you'll ride with the remainder of your company half a mile behind the regiment as a rear guard. Keep a steady distance. Captain McQuestion will select ten troopers to stay with me in case I need them to carry messages. Your men are all to carry their full issue of ammunition in their pockets, not on their horses—if a man's unhorsed, I don't want him disarmed by it. Captain Harris, I'll be keeping your troop in reserve when we begin the attack, since your men were up during the storm guarding the horses. All right, mount them up."

Mallory stood fast while the others walked to their troops. A man came up the hill with Mallory's horse. Mallory climbed into the bite of the frozen saddle leather. He turned the horse around and had a look at the four troopers whose spades were bent against the ice-hard ground, trenching a grave for Van De Reuter. There was no one near enough to see Mallory's expression.

# 13

Mallory lay on his belly at the long crest of the ridge. He waved Justin Harris forward, and when Harris crawled up, Mallory handed the field glasses to him and said, "Let's see how much you've learned. Take a look. Tell me how you'd do it."

Justin Harris spoke while he focused the binoculars. "This is no chess game, Colonel."

"You may find some interesting parallels."

The air was dismally cold. Clouds made an alternating pattern across the sky. Harris moved the glasses up in a slow turn, sweeping the valley. It lay stretched out like a naked, unsuspecting woman.

At the lower end, nearest him, he saw standing an old Spanish church. One of its domes was gone, perhaps never completed. Part was whitewashed; some of it was in great bare patches of brown where the plaster had peeled away. The air was still enough to carry a few sounds up to Harris: the distant thrum of a horse galloping in a tight circle on the end of a rope where an Apache was training it; the scratch of stone from an earth-flat where a woman was scraping a hide.

The rancherias lay strung out: three villages dotted down the length of the mountain meadow. The ground pitched up into spire-timbered slopes. The tilt of the valley was upward toward the farther end. A cloud curled over a clearing high on the opposite mountain. Fires burned in the three rancherias. Huts were thatched, wickiup style, made of brush and branches— whatever came to hand. Animal skins hung out drying on wooden frames among the *jacals*. An old man sat in the sun, warming his hands over a fire. The villages seemed busy with activity, Indians in all manner of costume threading the streetless encampments.

It was perhaps not quite two miles to the far end of the valley. It was open; there was no way to come up unseen. Perhaps it had been chosen with that in mind.

Mallory's voice startled him. "Well?"

Harris said, "I can't tell how many fighting men they've got."

"Rubio thinks there may be as many as two hundred."

"Then we haven't got them outnumbered. I'd feel better if we were up to strength. Well, it seems to me you've got only one way to do it. If you start at one end, that's no good. By the time you fight through the first and second villages, they'll either escape out the far end or make a massed stand at the third village. You've got to bottle up both ends."

"Go on."

"I guess I'd divide into three companies and set one against each village, all three attacks at the same time."

When the colonel did not answer, Harris put down the field

glasses and looked at him. Mallory's aspect was bleak. "I'm afraid I haven't taught you very much."

"You didn't have much of a student."

"Your idea is bad. Do you know why?"

"No."

"They'd want us to do that. They'd like to split us into three small groups and butcher us one by one. In a case like this, Captain, you keep your strength gathered together. I'll put one troop at the far end of the valley to prevent a wholesale escape from that end. The remainder of the regiment will attack in force. I intend to sweep straight up from the foot of the valley."

"I see," Justin Harris said. "And it'll be Ben Hannibal's troop that will have to hold the far end of it, alone."

"Yes."

"For God's sake, it's suicide for him. He'll be cut to pieces."

"He'll suffer heavy casualties, but he'll hold. His men will hold. We'll lose fewer men than we would by dividing into three."

"But you're picking the men who'll die!"

Mallory said, after a time, "Go back to your post, Captain."

Ben Hannibal felt chilled through. He touched the half-healed scar on his earlobe from the Weaver's Canyon fight. He sat his horse at the edge of the regiment and felt blood race through him. He felt weak; his hand trembled; his mouth was dry. A horse sneezed, and the sound all but propelled him away. He had the afternoon sun at the back of his right shoulder; its rays sliced down without warmth through clouds left behind by the storm.

Behind him the ragged line of men extended in double rank, stirrup to stirrup along the uneven backside of the ridge. Up and over—the regiment would climb twenty feet, bolt over the top, and charge down. Mallory trotted over and spoke in a loud voice so that all of them would hear.

"Don't shoot women and don't shoot children. Be careful of your targets—they may have white prisoners or Mexicans. We're not here to butcher. I don't want this written down as another Chivington massacre."

Mallory wheeled his horse alongside Ben Hannibal's and said more quietly, "We'll come up as quickly as we can. Lieutenants

Sandin and Merriweather will pull away from the regiment at the first village and hold it after we have charged through. They'll clean out the huts and corrals, round up prisoners, and hold the positions. Lieutenants Burbridge and Couts will do the same at the second village. The remainder of us will go straight on into the third village to meet you. Let me give you a word or two of advice. Concentrate at first on their horse herds. Find them and detail a strong party of men to them. That's where the Indians will head first when we begin the attack. You'll see us coming, I expect, if you've time to look for us. We will drive down the valley in two columns, attempting to keep them between us to prevent escape. Captain Harris will close up the rear as we move forward. We've got a mile and a half to run, and I've given my men instructions to conserve their horses. The attack will be at the gallop down the hill into the first village, but thereafter we'll keep down to the canter. One thing —in case I am killed or put out of action, Captain McQuestion is to assume command." Mallory was looking across the distance of a hundred yards at Justin Harris. "Do you understand exactly what you're to do, Lieutenant?"

Ben Hannibal had to place his hand on the saddle pommel to keep the tremor from showing. Mallory said crisply, "You will take a position above the last village, and you will hold that position at all costs until we arrive to support you. There will be no question of retreat."

Ben Hannibal watched him unblinkingly. Mallory said, "Good luck, mister," and gave him a quick salute and rode off. Pete Rubio rode to intercept the colonel, still within earshot of Ben Hannibal, and Hannibal heard Rubio say, "You ever get a chance to use that fishing pole I give you?"

"I'm afraid not," Mallory said, riding right on.

"That's too bad," Rubio said, and swung his horse away.

Ben Hannibal thought, don't shoot women, don't shoot kids. But in a wild galloping fight how did you distinguish your target? It was cold, damnably cold. The altitude was high, and the storm had left a vacuum behind. He could see bodies jerking and jaws chattering down the line. The flesh of his chest rippled in a chilled tremor. He saw Cpl. Boone Blockman's round, hot eyes lying flat against the colonel, far down the slope; Blockman's words were loud enough for everyone to hear:

"Son-of-a-bitch ain't going to do to me what he done to my brother. He ain't getting no puking chance." Ben Hannibal thought about that and remembered Van De Reuter.

In the rock jaws the horses bunched themselves, and Ben Hannibal saw Mallory draw his revolver from the back-flap holster to inspect it. The bugler had his bugle up, but Mallory waved him back. The resentful sun poured down. Pete Rubio came scrambling along the slope, hunched over on foot, and dropped to talk to a captain not far away. "Soon as you go over the hill, you'll see an old mission church. Horse herd's right behind it. That's your target—a little left of dead center. All right?" And went on without waiting an answer.

Down the line, faces lifted, bright and anxious, afraid; the lackluster weariness had been driven from them all. Mallory sat his horse, off a bit from the regiment, alone. Ben Hannibal flung a quick look, half of terror, at Justin Harris. Harris was turned away. The phrase rang through Ben Hannibal, *at all costs*. He caught Mallory's hand signal and turned, nodding; he glimpsed Justin Harris looking at him.

Justin Harris looked across fifteen yards of rock and saw Ben Hannibal's face—taut, white, lips drawn back in a strained parody of a grin. Ben Hannibal appeared to shrink. Harris was shocked down to his belly by the raw look in Ben Hannibal's eyes. It was like that of a starving child.

Ben Hannibal led his troop out, filing past Harris across the back of the hill, going down to the far end a mile and a half distant and taking his position there. Watching them go down, Harris recognized their faces: Bodeen, Crane, Blockman, Hoag. Harris looked at his own sergeant. He rubbed the grips of his revolver to warm them, and he took six cartridges from his ammunition pouch and held them in the circle of his fist, threading the reins through the fingers. His stomach slowly knotted. It was bitter cold, and he had a few wry thoughts. What a hell of a Christmas. He envisioned a Christmas dinner laid out on white linen. The metal butt strap of his new Smith & Wesson revolver was so cold his fingers stuck to it. His lip was split from dry, cold wind; it stung painfully when he licked at it. He tugged his hat down tight and saw the sergeant dragging the back of a sleeve across his mouth.

An Agency Indian scout was on the ridge, lying flat, watching the rancherias through field glasses. The scout wormed backward off the skyline and trotted to Mallory and spoke briefly. Mallory's hat came off in his gloved hand, and his white hair gleamed frosty silver. A trooper then raised the guidon. Wind pulled it out straight, a lettered blue pennant with twin-breasted barbs, trimmed in gold. A crystal rime lay on the rocks, and ice was a glaze in the shadowed crevices. Funnels of mist hung before every man's open breathing mouth.

Colonel Mallory tossed his hat five feet in the air. Before it came down, Ben Hannibal's troop was in motion, over the top and out of sight. From that end of the ridge came a dotting of gunfire; Hannibal was engaged.

There was no bugle, no cry—there was only Mallory's silent signal. The blue line kicked forward. Horses scrambled to the ridge, plunged over, and galloped. Mallory's hair streamed in the wind, a white beacon. The regiment gathered like a fan, breaking from formation into a column as it swept down the tilt. The column split in two, and both of its legs ran in files of four, sprawled back like ropes. Wind stretched the guidon and flapped it roughly. Hoofs scattered the thin crust of snow.

Indians in the valley came erect and spun toward their weapons. The regiment made an intense racket, the pound of iron on rock; men lay forward along their bounding saddles. Horses ran downhill at breakneck speed, carried by the momentum of the charge. Now and then a trooper shouted. Cold air burned their throats. Before they were halfway to the first village, the place was festooned with muzzle flame. The columns drew apart to a separation of a hundred yards and held that distance, Mallory leading one, McQuestion the other; Mallory's was the first to come within range of the Indian marksmen. The valley was alive with gunfire.

At the far end of the valley Ben Hannibal swirled through the rocks, fighting his horse down; a bullet had singed its withers. He shouted along the hill, "Prepare to fight on foot. Horse holders."

Bodeen and Trooper Hoag raced up afoot and took their stands with him, in the boulders near the Indian horses. He saw his men bellying down in the rocks, seeking firing positions.

Indians ran around in the village, confused, hardly battling yet, but keeping up an unsteady volley of shots. Ben Hannibal said, "Calm down—pick them off." He stood behind a tall rock, one hand braced on it. "Crane, get your head down!"

Corporal Blockman was worming down with a grim set to his face, holding his fire. A stray bullet chipped rock near Trooper Hoag, and Hoag commenced cursing in his thin, high voice. Bodeen growled at him. "Cut that out—cut that out." Trooper Crane dropped and clung flat behind a rock, hiding, watching Ben Hannibal with bright eyes. The cold rolled up in Ben Hannibal's face. Apaches ran through the village, seeking leadership: half were not armed. Along the slope Ben Hannibal's troopers laid down a pulse of fire.

Mallory's soldiers racked into the first village, guns up. Someone was shouting hysterically in long wails. Twenty or thirty thin spirals of cookfire smoke rose from roof holes in the wickiups. Indian women, caught in the open, dropped their work and scuttled to cover. Sergeant Major McCracken, with his hat jammed down to his eyes, leaped his horse over a stack of pelts and ran past the side of the old church. Mallory wheeled into the village, white hair shining, a clean target. A gunshot exploded bright in his face but missed him. The air was full of the boom of powder.

Halfway down the run, Justin Harris halted his company in a milling circle to hold them in reserve. He had a view of the entire field of action. He spoke harshly. "Spread out—four ranks and flankers. Form up!"

He saw the banner of Mallory's mane leading the swarm of cavalry through the disorder of the camp. Mallory's arm chopped up and down; Mallory stopped; his horse reared and turned full around. He called out steady commands and watched the movements of his flankers, dispatching squads of men here and there. The valley sloped up in patches of rock and snow and puffs of powder smoke. Harris held his men in check and saw the sway and fog of battle far upvalley, where Ben Hannibal's small force contained the massing Apaches. The racket was intense. In the first village Harris caught sight of Mallory, rallying men around weak points, driving forward at an incredible rate and somehow keeping his line intact.

Harris moved his troop forward against the edge of the village, enclosing the rear. His men began to find targets. The camp teemed with scuttling figures. Ahead the guidon went down. Colonel Mallory scooped it up from the saddle and pressed the guidon into the hands of the first trooper galloping by. Harris had the sudden knowledge that in spite of anything it was Mallory they followed now; it was Mallory they looked to and watched.

"A" Troop ran down the right side of the village, firing concertedly: a crowd of Indians was running afoot toward some horses and "A" rammed on to intercept them. Harris, wheeling that way to cut the Apaches off, felt the telescoped confusion of the charge. An old Apache with one arm tied down in a bandage came out of a *jacal*, brandishing a spear. Harris's bullet cut him down in his tracks.

A knot of braves gathered in the rancheria, forming a ring of defensive riflery. In glimpses Harris had images of a fierce battle over there beyond the church. Rifles boomed from within the mission itself. Half of Lieutenant Merriweather's troop dismounted to take cover and return the fire from the church. A brown woman ran out of a hut with a small child by the hand. The woman yelled defiance; a trooper's horse knocked her down, rushing over her.

Breaking loose, a pack of riderless ponies ran through the rancheria. One Apache, carrying rifle and bandolier, made a running leap to the back of a pony racing with the bunch. His legs locked around its barrel, and the Indian raised his rifle. Firing, knee-turning the horse, the Indian ran in and out of Justin Harris's sight and crossed almost the entire length of the village before a bullet from the ground cut the horse out and the Indian sprawled, his rifle somersaulting away. A mounted trooper ran over the Indian, trampling him; the last Harris saw of him the Indian was lurching away, dragging one leg, seeking either cover or a weapon.

Rifle fire issued in sheets from the church. Lieutenant Sandin committed his entire troop against it, dismounting and reinforcing Merriweather's beleaguered men. The chatter of Indian rifles, crackling sharply across the thin air, was met by the hollow, deafening boom of the issue carbines.

There was no dust. The air was diamond-sharp and fogged

only by stinging drifts of sulphur smoke. Out of the chaotic spinning Drew Mallory's pattern began to take shape in Harris's vision. Keeping abreast of the fanned columns, Mallory smashed into the second village while Merriweather and Sandin and Harris consolidated the first. Harris's men moved slowly along like a broom, missing nothing, pushing stragglers into a vise. He dismounted half of them and sent them into the huts.

Mallory could be seen from almost anywhere, a white mace swinging up and down. Harris had glimpses of him while the troop closed up the rear and pried reluctant Apaches out of wickiups.

Higher in the valley, Ben Hannibal's troop made their stand in the rocks, separated still by almost a mile from the main force. They held, a fragile line half obscured by their own smoke. Boone Blockman cursed while he fired, and Trooper Hoag fumbled cartridges. Sergeant Bodeen was down on one knee, picking his targets with cool deliberation; often, like a bitch watching its litter, he ran from point to point and gave strength where it was needed. Ben Hannibal cocked his revolver and stared through the smoke with red eyes.

The Apaches came up out of the village in a quick swarm. Forty yards distant they dropped flat to aim. Trooper Crane broke out of his petrified fear and lifted his rifle. The dusty curl of smoke bloomed around Ben Hannibal, and he had to move aside to see if his bullets had struck true. He wished bitterly for another fifty soldiers. He saw men going down—Tompkins, shot in the face; Stein, with no visible wound, going over with a jerk of the neck and a flap of the arms like a dead turkey. One man was getting to his knees stubbornly, bleeding at the right shoulder; the man shifted his carbine around to fire it left-handed. Bodeen, crawling by, stopped and pushed the man down and made some kind of bandage for him—all the while firing his revolver at steady intervals.

Ben Hannibal watched it all from a point of suspension. The fight had a distant unreality; he could not find his own presence in it. He felt nauseated and drained. The Indians advanced toward his line, crawling on their bellies, presenting very poor targets. All the time there were more of them coming out of the village. The blast of guns was steady. It became dull in Ben Hannibal's ears. He felt a bullet lash past his face. The soldier who was firing one-handed with his left hand dropped his carbine and cried out and fell to one side. Bodeen stepped into the man's position and slashed his shots downhill.

An increased thudding of carbines came up the valley, and Ben Hannibal saw the lunging white hair break out of the second village. Everyone saw Mallory, and a shout went up, overriding the chop of gunfire. Ben Hannibal swung his head around, angry with white heat; his eyes fell on a trooper sitting up against a rock with one hand across his stomach, his face loose and his eyes glazed.

A group of Indians got to their feet. They slashed up toward the left flank of Ben Hannibal's line. All through the rocks Springfields turned to beat back the Indians. Three Apaches dropped; the others shrank back. The troop's savage fire drove them half the distance back to the village, and a second shout went up among the troopers. Drew Mallory was clearly visible, galloping forward a foolhardy distance ahead of his charging columns. The call lifted and hung, ringing with echoes through the rocks. Trooper Crane, with a yell on his lips, pulled the trigger and dropped an Indian in his tracks.

A thunder of men bent and shot and swayed, horses wheeling and exploding, hoofs tossing up clots of earth and snow, the brassy yelling of men, the angry whoops of others. Mallory reached the third village and stopped, waiting for his men to come up. A bullet struck him in the arm somewhere and turned him half around in the saddle, but Mallory kept his seat and lifted his revolver to fire. The regiment ran into the village, and Ben Hannibal stepped forward into plain view. His voice chimed through the noise. "Line of skirmishers—come *on!*"

He started walking downslope and had not taken three paces when the troopers rose from the rocks and made a line to either side that stretched across the hillside. Powder snow boiled up. The Indians sat back on their heels to take the attack. Ben Hannibal's revolver rocked and bucked against his palm. Smoke put tears in his eyes.

The first cavalryman broke through the village; his horse bucked him off. Shot through the lungs, the horse vomited purple foam and whirled away through the rancheria. Echoes beat out more thickly. An Apache roared out of a hut, rolled like a cat on the ground to avoid the hoofs of a riderless horse, and came up on one knee with a repeating rifle; the Indian held his ground there, with a woman and two small children in the hut behind him, until finally a trooper shot him down. The woman erupted from the hut with a knife: she leaped on the trooper, slashing his arm. The trooper kicked her away and ran on, bleeding.

Trooper Hoag was the first of Ben Hannibal's men to reach the third village. All order had broken in the columns. Hoag cried through the turmoil, ran into the village, and began to pepper Indians, who were running in every direction. A knife buried itself hilt-deep in Hoag's chest; he flopped down.

A tawny Indian loomed before Ben Hannibal, and he shot the man down and uttered a husky laugh.

An Indian horse ran through the valley, dragging its entrails; its belly had been laid open by a knife or spear.

A narrow ditch crossed part of the third village. Five troopers, trying to jump on labored horses, were pitched headlong from their mounts when the horses plunged into the ditch. One of the horses ran around with the bone of a broken leg protruding from its hide. Mallory was in the village center, his arm raised, calling for order. No one heard his voice, but his lips could be seen moving. He gathered a body of men around him and began to smash through the huts. All down the valley troopers rolled around in constant motion. The church was taken; soldiers fired now from the bell tower. A squad ran through that first village, setting huts on fire. Infants crawled around squawling.

Singly and in small knots, Apaches gave resistance. A number of them tried running up the sides of the valley into the trees, and some made it. Others lay on the slopes. Lieutenant Sandin's men corraled women, who spat and shouted and gestured toward the troopers. A number of women ran away; no one made great effort to stop them. In the second village Lieutenant Couts ran up and down firing his revolver indiscriminately toward a swelling circle of Apache fighters making a final stand. Inevitably a bullet reached Lieutenant Couts and knocked him down.

Mallory established a command post at the outer edge of the third village and dispatched riders to his officers. Bleeding from one arm, Mallory sat bolt upright on his horse and fired when he saw an Indian within revolver range. Lt. Will Sandin came up through the village on foot, a wiry bantam figure watching Mallory with awe. Shots from an adobe-and-straw hut brought down Drew Mallory's horse; he spilled off, rolled away, and commandeered a trooper s horse. Three men poured bullets into the hut doorway. The Apache pitched outward.

Will Sandin reloaded his revolver with fevered haste and ran around looking for a horse; he felt naked on foot. A little child ran toward him, yelling in a high, piping voice. The child leaped on him and tried to take his revolver away. He threw the child off and wheeled in time to see Cpl. Boone Blockman running forward. Blockman was coming down behind Drew Mallory; Blockman's face was wild; his carbine was lifting.

There was a tremendous careering of shots and shouting—a battle at the far end of the village. Blockman stopped and shouldered his carbine to aim. Sandin lifted his revolver. He braced himself to shout, but no sound came from his lips; he did not move. Blockman was set to fire at Mallory when Sergeant Major McCracken waddled into sight beside a hut and blasted Blockman through the stomach with a revolver charge. Blockman's carbine thundered. The bullet plowed the earth beneath Mallory's plunging horse. The horse jumped, but Mallory kept his seat; he turned and saw Will Sandin, face flushed, crouching before an Indian hut with an upraised revolver. McCracken walked forward, and Boone Blockman folded down like a sick man over his wounded belly. Blockman fell on his face and gasped for breath.

McCracken said to Sandin, "Why the hell didn't you shoot?" Sandin shook his head mutely. The sergeant major walked over to Blockman and deliberately shot the corporal through the head. Drew Mallory rode his horse up and spoke to Sandin. "Lieutenant, you are finished in this regiment."

A group of Indians were fortified in a ditch beyond the village, and Captain McQuestion, who enjoyed nothing so much as a fight, had gathered a band of men to carry the battle to them; he lined his troopers up and led them in a charge against the ditch. Four troopers went down in the run. The rest of them cleared the ditch in a jump, firing straight down on the Indians as they went over. Blood ran down the ditch. A few Apaches left alive surrendered to McQuestion.

What remained of the fight were ragged aftervolleys, individual combat. A skirmish was concentrated around the horse herd of the last village, where fifteen Apaches made a game attempt to reach their animals. Ben Hannibal had four troopers with the herd; he led a quickly gathered squad forward on the Indians' flank. A bullet made a track across the top of his shoulder; he shifted the revolver to his left hand and kept walking forward.

The Apaches were strung out in a loose, crouching line. Ben Hannibal's squad ran out in front, scattering before the herd to intercept the Indians. Trooper Crane cried out valiantly and rushed up to take a stand beside Ben Hannibal. Ben Hannibal called to his men and began to walk ahead, firing. Indians bobbed up and down before him, and he chopped his revolver at them angrily, flinging out bullets with quick abandon.

A shot punched through Trooper Crane's temple, showering Ben Hannibal with blood. Crane dropped like a plumb weight. Ben Hannibal said, "Oh, God—oh, Jesus." He picked up Crane's revolver and ran toward the Indians, punching out cartridges. Rifle fire sang out from the troopers behind him, and the Apache line faltered, broke, and scrambled away. Ben Hannibal shot two Indians in the back. His head rocked when each of them fell. He was breathing in jerks. His sights found an Indian woman crossing the hummock, and he fired, missed, and fired again. The woman tumbled out of sight. He took aim on another warrior and pulled the trigger with violent elation. The revolver was empty, and he cursed it. Indians stood up, hands in the air, glaring at him and his troopers. Ben Hannibal lashed them with oaths and waved his men forward to accept their surrender. A dying Indian lay at his feet, and he took a chop at the man's head with his revolver.

Smoke lifted along the valley; Justin Harris's men walked through the villages, setting them afire. Flames drove Indians out of hiding, and the troopers captured them or shot them. The brush *jacals* and thatched roofs caught fire with explosions like powder kegs. Ammunition left inside the huts went off like fireworks.

Mallory stood on a high point of ground and waved the regimental bugler forward. "Sound recall."

# 14

Captain McQuestion emerged from the smoke on horseback. Mallory said, "Have you found Togomasai?"

"Dead."

"How many escaped?"

"Not more than a dozen. They're broken, I think—we'll be having no more trouble from down here."

McQuestion went on to his troopers. Dotted figures moved through the villages, now and then shooting. Smoke climbed in black expanding spheres, shadowing the rancherias. Sergeant Major McCracken came along, and Mallory said to him, "Get me a report of casualties. Gather the prisoners to the left of the village on that open piece of ground. Where's the surgeon?"

"Up there someplace," McCracken said, tilting his head toward the first village. Someone was ringing the church bell. There was a ragged tattoo of gunfire. McCracken said, "Lieutenant Couts is dead, sir. Found him by the lower ditch."

"Get moving, Sergeant Major."

McCracken rubbed his paunch and went. Occasional shots continued to rip the air. Horse holders came down with Ben Hannibal's mounts. The cough of a Springfield carbine barked nearby. The regiment dismounted and began to form up. "A" Troop followed Harris's men in a last tidying sweep through the burning villages. The stink of charred cowhide and horse skins became thick. Coughing became a more common sound than shooting. A ring of troopers linked arms around the growing gather of Apache prisoners. Clayton, the surgeon, ran around with his bag, exhorting troopers to make litters and travois and gather the wounded in one place. Officers straggled up to report to Mallory.

When Ben Hannibal arrived, Mallory said, "I saw you beat off that last Indian run, Lieutenant. Foolhardy, but well done."

Ben Hannibal only looked at him out of red, dismal eyes; he turned on his heel and walked down into the burning rancherias. Mallory watched him disappear behind the smoke pyre of a half-consumed wickiup. It was then for the first time that uncertainty struck Mallory, and he was puzzled.

They carried the corpse of Corporal Blockman past him, and Lieutenant Sandin walked with it. Sandin's frightened eyes lifted to Mallory's and fell away. Sandin said, "He wanted revenge for a brother he had."

"I know all about that," Mallory said. "Get out of my sight, Lieutenant."

A single pistol shot punched the smoke-heavy air. It seemed to come from within the village. Justin Harris, who had been walking into the village, began to run. Mallory looked that way. Presently Harris emerged from the smoke, his face ghostly pale. Mallory had a premonition. Harris walked straight to him and said, "Colonel, if you'd come down this way?" And walked back toward the village without waiting an answer.

Someone behind Mallory cried wretchedly. Someone else said "Happy Christmas, you bastards!" Mallory did not look around. He walked after Harris. He went through a stinging pall of smoke and batted through it and found Harris outlined in the dark acrid fog.

Ben Hannibal lay crumpled behind a burning hut. His eyes were open, but he was dead, a bullet hole in his temple and part of the top of his head blown away.

Harris stood by Ben Hannibal's splayed feet, very grim and very taut. Mallory said carefully, "See any Indians around here, Captain?"

"I can't say."

"That's a powder burn on the wound."

"Is it?" Harris's face was inscrutable.

"Shot point-blank," Mallory said, as if he meant to force himself to face everything. He looked down and saw that Ben Hannibal's revolver was buttoned down inside its holster. Mallory tugged it out and snapped open the loading-gate. "Reloaded recently and one shot fired." He looked up. His eyes were half shuttered, and he said deliberately, "Did you put his gun away in the holster, Captain?"

Harris did not speak. Mallory put the revolver away where he had gotten it and stood up. Then he crouched again, took out the revolver, and opened the gate. He punched out the fired cartridge and reloaded that chamber. Afterward he buttoned the weapon in its holster and got up and made a ritual dusting off of his hands. "All right. I'll keep your secret. He was a weak man."

"Was he?"

"He fought gallantly. It's best that the regiment believe he was killed by an Indian."

Harris said, "You're thinking about the rest of the men. What about him? What about Ben Hannibal?"

Drew Mallory bared his teeth. "He was a fool."

"You've made a lie of him. Do you think he'd want to be remembered as a battle hero, for God's sake?"

"If a man lives by a lie, he's got to be able to die by it. I intend to put him in for the Medal of Honor."

"You have no soul at all," Harris cried.

A shaft of bright sunlight pierced the smoke and shone on Mallory's white hair, smudged and smoke-grayed. Justin Harris stepped across Hannibal's body and gripped Mallory's coat; he shouted, "Do you still think this is a God-damned chess game?" His face was chalky with the tracks of sweat and smoke. Great fires crackled and roared. Harris cried, "You wanted a gold star for them to follow—but he was only fool's gold, and you knew it when you tried to make him into your image. You wanted him to be the star, but all the time you were the star they followed, not him." Harris's voice rose unreasonably. "You didn't have to destroy him! Was he a pawn?"

Mallory's face was gaunt and hollowed. A cavalry bandanna, knotted about his arm, stirred in the wind. He did not speak. He swung with a snap of his trim shoulders and was absorbed into the curling smoke.

Justin Harris looked down upon Ben Hannibal. Rage gave way. A remote elusive expression touched his face. He passed a hand over his eyes; a knotted muscle rippled at his jaw. Cold winds swept across the mountains, and the smoke was colored red by the flames that fed it.

Once: Winner of Spur Award for

## BEST WESTERN SHORT STORY
## DOROTHY M. JOHNSON

Twice: Winners of Spur Awards for

## BEST WESTERN NOVEL

## LEE LEIGHTON and
## ELMER KELTON

Three
Times: Winners of Spur Awards for

## BEST WESTERN HISTORICAL

## LUCIA MOORE
## FRED GROVE and
## E. E. HALLERAN

---

Ballantine Books authors lead the country in the writing of modern Westerns, with real people facing real difficulties against backgrounds of the West which are totally authentic.

**Write for our complete catalog to Ballantine Books, 36 West 20th Street, New York, New York 10003**

# Western Adventure
## from
## Wade Everett

**FORT STARKE**

**TEXAS RANGER**

**TOP HAND**

**BIG MAN, BIG MOUNTAIN**

**TEMPORARY DUTY**

**LAST SCOUT**

Uniformly priced at 50¢
(plus 5¢ per book mailing cost)